D1385571

No Buts, Becky!

No Buts, Becky!

by José Patterson
Illustrated by Patricia Drew

Matador
9 Priory Business Park,
Wistow Road, Kibworth Beauchamp,
Leicestershire. LE8 0RX
Tel: (+44) 116 279 2299
Fax: (+44) 116 279 2277
Email: books@troubador.co.uk
Web: www.troubador.co.uk/matador

ISBN 978 1780884 387 (paperback)
978 1780884 394 (hardback)

British Library Cataloguing in Publication Data.
A catalogue record for this book is available from the British Library.

Typeset by Troubador Publishing Ltd, Leicester, UK

Matador is an imprint of Troubador Publishing Ltd

Printed and bound in the UK by TJ International, Padstow, Cornwall

For David

and for my grandchildren

Michael, Emily, Louis, Sally, Raphi, Oscar, Felix and Lily.

Acknowledgements

I am indebted to my special friend Jackie Finlay, without whose unflagging help *No Buts, Becky!* would not have been published and to Patricia Drew for her delightful illustrations.

Chapter 1

When Becky's mother was alive, she taught her that the Yiddish words *'oy vey'* do not only mean 'oh dear.'

They can also mean trouble. Becky was quite sure that the tall, strange man was trouble. Why else did just one look at him make her break out in goosebumps? He wasn't family, so why was he here? Something else happened only this morning which was an even worse kind of *oy vey*. Bubbe, her Grandmother, suddenly announced, "I'm getting too old and sick to look after you and Yossie. You need a new mother, and what's more, your father agrees with me." *A new mother!* Just like that: no warning: three terrible words. Her mouth had gone dry and she had stood, shocked and shaking, listening to her heart thumping. What did Bubbe mean and what exactly had her father agreed to?

Becky watched the stranger *schmoozing* and fussing around Bubbe. What was he doing here? she asked herself again. She didn't trust him one little bit.

"Good *Shabbos*, good *Shabbos*, Mrs Feldman," he gushed, repeating the traditional Jewish Sabbath greeting to Bubbe. "What a great honour it is to be here. Jacob, my friend," he nodded at Becky's father, "God has blessed you with two wonderful children. Ah! Yossie, Yossie," he crooned, patting the boy's head, "your grandmother tells me that you're learning to read Hebrew and studying the Torah – God's holy law – so you'll be a great rabbi when you're a man. Such pride and joy for your family."

Becky felt sorry for her little brother who squirmed with embarrassment. 'He's only just eight years old and he doesn't want to be a rabbi,' she wanted to tell everyone, but she didn't dare. *Please God*, she prayed, *don't let that man start on me.*

"And as for your daughter, Becky," the stranger smirked, "what a lucky man you are Jacob, to have such a pretty daughter."

Me – pretty? *Me* with frizzy hair? *Me* with my lopsided nose? Becky had to bite her tongue to stop herself answering back. *He's not blind,* Becky thought, *he can see perfectly well that I'm plain, always have been, for all of my ten years in fact. He's just schmoozing again to get round Papa.*

Friday night, the beginning of the Sabbath, was different from the rest of the week. The table was covered with a white cloth used only on *Shabbos*. In the centre, two candles flickered gently in the polished brass candlesticks. Next to them was a bottle of special wine and two *challahs* – plaited poppy seed loaves. The water in the Russian samovar kettle bubbled quietly. The gas light hissed gently, making little plopping, spluttering sounds. Its burning gas-jet heated the small, white gauze cover until it glowed, sending shimmering beams of light dancing across the shabby room. A fire crackled cheerfully in the grate behind the iron bars of the black cooking range. Papa poured out the wine, recited the Sabbath blessings, sprinkled salt on the slices of challah, and handed them round.

Becky bit her lips to stop them trembling. Friday night was the time she missed her mother the most. Not just the hugs and kisses and all the bits of gossip she'd heard, but the way Mama always encouraged her. "My Becky," she would say with a smile, "is going to be a scholarship girl, you'll see. Everyone should be blessed with such a clever daughter." It was only a year since she had died. Papa had been sad and silent for hours on end. Family, friends and neighbours had brought food and comfort. Then Bubbe had moved in to look after them.

Becky looked across at her brother. She knew that Bubbe's news had upset him. On their way to school this morning, he had stopped suddenly and looked at her with his big, dark eyes.

"Becky, what did Bubbe mean when she said we needed a new mother?"

She gave him a quick hug.

"Take no notice, Yossie," she had told him. "You know what Bubbe's like when she's trying to get all the work done before *Shabbos*. She nearly bit my head off this morning when I accidentally knocked over her cup of tea. Don't worry about it, okay?"

But she couldn't forget it. *A new mother*! – those words haunted her. She couldn't concentrate on anything else, in or out of school.

Becky looked round the table. Bubbe was fussing over

her guest, Yossie was hungry – as always, even Papa managed a smile or two. *Everyone seems happy enough*, she thought, *except me*. Becky wished she knew what Bubbe and Papa were planning; she hated being the last to know everything. Why when she desperately wanted to talk to her Papa did he invite this strange, *schmoozing* man who gabbled away all the time and made her head ache? She wondered what her mama would have thought of it. *If only…* she chewed her lip slowly as an idea flashed into her mind.

★ ★ ★

Flat 74 Rothschild Buildings,
Brick Lane,
Whitechapel,
London.

Friday 6ᵗʰ November 1908

Dear Mama,

If only I could write to you and send my letter straight to Heaven! I'm not allowed to write because it's Shabbos, so instead I'll do it inside my head.

My lovely teacher, Miss Bennet, taught us how to write a proper letter today. The address goes first, then the date which is Friday, 6th November, 1908, then 'Dear Somebody or Other' ending with 'Yours faithfully.' "Who can we write to, Miss?" one of the children asked her.

"Your family and friends for a start," Miss Bennet said. "Why, you could even send a letter to the king of England, but I would like to see your handwriting improve first. It would be a pity if King Edward V11 can't read what you've written, wouldn't it?"

Rothschild Buildings is just the same. Old Mrs Galinsky in flat 35 is going mad. The other day she leant over the banisters and yelled at Yossie. "You, boy, you there, stop whistling. It's bad luck! You'll call up the devil!" Then guess what! Her false teeth – just the top set – fell out of her mouth and dropped right down the stairwell! I made Yossie go in quickly before he got the giggles, and I found her teeth – a bit slimy, ugh! – and gave them back to her. I had to look away when she put them back in!

I still go to take our cholent pot to Mr Marston the baker every Friday afternoon. He loves having his little joke. He lifted the cholent pot lid, peeped in, pretended to taste it and said it was not only the most delicious beef stew in Rothschild Buildings, but in the whole of the East End of London!! I don't suppose, like me, he's ever been to the West End of London, or else he would have included it! Then he gave me a metal tag with a number on it, put the matching one on the handle of the pot and pushed it to the back of the oven with a long handled paddle to cook overnight. Then guess what? He told me he had heard that I'm a big help to Bubbe and gave me a piece of cake. Wasn't that kind of him?

Bubbe's been in a funny mood and snaps at me for the most little thing. I think the pain in her legs make her grumpy. She drove me mad when we went shopping in the market yesterday. She kept poking and prodding the chickens. This one was too scraggy, that one too fatty. I thought she'd never make up her mind!

Papa's Shabbos guest was cross-eyed with thick bushy eyebrows which shot up and down very quickly when he spoke! I know he can't help it but it's very difficult to talk to someone like that because you don't know which eye to look at. His coat wasn't very clean and he had a red handkerchief in his top pocket. He kept stroking his beard and smiling and nodding and schmoozing. He made such loud slurping noises when he drank his chicken soup that Yossie got the giggles and Papa sent him out of the room.

5

Now – I'm going to share the 'Secrets Of My Heart' with you. I read that somewhere and I think it sounds lovely! I don't think Miss Bennet would think so but I don't care – I'm going to tell you! Bubbe's chicken soup is very good but not nearly as good as yours!

I hope you are happy up there with God. I love you very much.

Yours faithfully,

Rebecca Feldman.

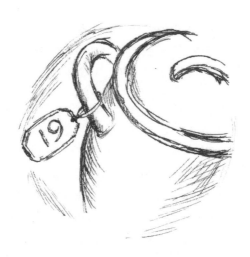

Chapter 2

A gentle tap on the front door woke Becky with a start.

"I'm Meg," the young girl said, twisting her apron nervously. "Me Mam's sick. She sent me to 'elp you."

"Come in, come in. It's too cold standing out there. My name is Rebecca, but everyone calls me Becky."

"You'll 'ave to tell me what to do, Becky, 'cos I've forgotten what Mam said."

"Course I will. Can you light the samovar?"

"The what?"

"The samovar – over there, it's like a big kettle."

Meg shook her head.

"See those bits of wood over there in the corner? You can use them. My father's a carpenter so he's allowed to bring some home. The charcoal's in that box and there's lots of old newspapers all over the place!"

Meg carefully followed all of Becky's instructions. She poured water into the samovar and emptied the little ash tray at the bottom. Then she crumpled up some paper and dropped it down the central tube. Carefully, she lit the paper, and slowly fed in thin sticks of wood, then thicker ones. As soon as they were burning well she added the charcoal.

"Well that's one job done," Meg said as she wiped her hands on her apron. "I'll make you a cup a tea when the water boils." She looked at the empty grate and shivered. "It's so cold in 'ere. I'd better light the fire before you freeze to death."

"Thanks Meg."

"That's better," Meg said later, sweeping up left over bits of wood. "Now that's what I call a good blaze."

"Mmm, lovely," Becky murmured, warming her hands.

Meg hesitated, then looked shyly at Becky and muttered, "I 'ope you don't think I'm being cheeky like, but…"

"I know what you're going to say," Becky butted in, "why am I standing here watching you work when I can just as easily do it myself – right?"

"I didn't mean to …" Meg looked embarrassed.

"It's okay. I can't do the chores today because it's *Shabbos*."

"What?"

"*Shabbos* is the Sabbath day, God's holy day of rest. Jewish people who are religious like us are forbidden to do any kind of work today – make a fire, or cook, or touch any money, or even write a letter. We have to go to *shul* and say our prayers.

"*Shul*?"

That's the Yiddish word for synagogue."

The bedroom door opened.

"Good *Shabbos*. Who's this? Where's Mrs Briggs?" Bubbe asked.

"She's sick. She sent her daughter, Meg."

Meg frowned. "Sorry, I don't understand what she's saying."

"We speak Yiddish at home or with friends. Bubbe doesn't know English very well. She's learning!" Becky grinned.

"She's not the only one! Honestly, Becky, I just don't know 'ow you manage to remember all them things you 'ave to do every *Shabbos*, and speak Yiddish as well. You're a bloomin' marvel, and no mistake!"

Becky flushed with pleasure. "My mother taught me lots of things. She would have been really proud of me to hear you say that."

Bubbe went into the kitchen and came back with a small parcel.

"Give zis to your mama" she said slowly in English. "Tell her, she should be well soon." Then she pointed to the few coins on the dresser.

"You take them," she said. "T'ank you."

"Thanks very much Mrs Feldman. Oh, and good *Shabbos*," she giggled.

"Becky, did you see that child?" Bubbe tut-tutted after Meg had left. "So pale and thin. Her poor mother has a hard life. Her husband spends most of his wages on drink, and hardly any on feeding his family. God help us if we can't find a little something to give to folks worse off than us. We're poor, it's true," she sighed, "but they're poorer."

"Bubbe, who was that strange man who came last night?" Becky asked.

Bubbe hesitated, "Papa met him in *shul* last night. He's lonely, poor man, so your father asked him to eat with us.

Why not? After all it's – a *mitzvah* – a good deed to have a *Shabbos* guest."

"But…"

"No buts, Becky. Call Papa and Yossie. We'll be late for *Shul*."

"No need, I'm here," Papa said quietly as he walked in. "Good *Shabbos*."

"Good *Shabbos*, Papa. Who was our guest last night?"

Her father's head was buried in his newspaper. Becky was nervous, but she went on.

"Has he just come from Russia?"

"For shame, Becky! Can't your papa have a cup of tea in peace without all these silly questions?"

"But …" Becky began, then stopped short.

"No buts, Becky," Papa frowned, "you heard what your grandmother said."

Becky had to bottle up her feelings of frustration. There were so many questions she wanted to ask, but she didn't dare. She knew better than to ignore her father's warning.

★ ★ ★

The synagogue was crowded. Papa and Yossie joined the men in the main part of the building and Becky helped Bubbe climb slowly upstairs to the women's section. The row of seats ran along three sides. The holy ark, where the Torah scrolls were kept, stood against the eastern wall.

Down below Becky could see the tops of the men's heads covered in hats and *kipas* – little skull caps – with their shoulders draped in prayer shawls. Suddenly she saw Yossie, who was sitting next to Papa. She couldn't see who was next to him until he too happened to look up. It was their *Shabbos* guest! Becky sat back in her seat, annoyed and upset. Then she felt something that didn't surprise her at all – another outbreak of goosebumps!

"You look as if you've got out of bed on the wrong side," a voice breathed in Becky's ear. This was followed by a quick hug and a kiss from Auntie Essie, her mother's sister. Becky opened her mouth to speak, but Auntie Essie placed a finger on her lips. "Later. It'll keep till later," she whispered.

Becky squeezed her hand. Auntie Essie was her favourite aunt. She never said, 'no buts.'

When all the Hebrew psalms and prayers came to an end, the Torah scroll was rolled up and draped in a velvet cloth. The *chazan* – the reader – carried it slowly, the tiny silver bells on top of the scroll handles tinkling as he moved along. Carefully, he lowered it into its place in the ark and closed the doors.

It was time for the rabbi to give his sermon. Becky was bored and didn't listen. Just then she noticed a lady sitting next to Bubbe. It was the way this woman smiled at Bubbe and patted her hand that made her feel uneasy.

★ ★ ★

"Becky, would you like to come home with me for a bite to eat?" Auntie Essie asked as soon as the service was over. "Yes? Good. I'll tell Bubbe."

Becky didn't have long to wait.

"Everything's settled," Auntie Essie told her. "Your father and Yossie will take Bubbe home, and if you give your tag to Mrs Kaminsky then she'll collect your cholent."

They left the worshippers calling 'Good *Shabbos*' to each other as they streamed out on to the road. It was cold and damp and a steady drizzle washed the pavements and

11

cobblestones. The Jewish shops were all closed for *Shabbos*, but for everyone else it was just another busy, crowded Saturday. There was a deafening roar from the traffic: tramcars, motor-buses, horse-buses, horses and carriages, carts and wagons of every shape and size.

"Here we are!" Auntie Essie puffed as she opened the door of her top floor apartment. "Take your wet things off, Becky darling, and warm yourself by the fire. What a godsend Lizzie is, lighting fires every *Shabbos* for all the Jewish families in this block. A real treasure!"

"We've got a new treasure, too, called Meg. It's so quiet here, Auntie Essie. Where is everyone?"

"Your Uncle Joe is visiting an old tailor friend of his who's very sick. Your cousins are with my sister-in-law and her family. They've promised to bring our cholent home later – if they remember. Here I am chatting away! Are you hungry?"

"Starving!"

"Good. The beetroots were going very cheap on the market yesterday which is why I decided to make them into soup. You know me for a bargain! So how about a bowl of soup and a slice or two of challah?"

"My mouth's watering already!"

"And to finish off," Essie said, tying her apron, "I've saved you a piece of apple cake. There's hardly ever any leftovers here, even the mice and cockroaches have a hard time!" she laughed. "Come, let's eat."

"Mmm! It's all so good," Becky said between mouthfuls.

"Well?" Auntie Essie asked, when they had finished and cleared the table. "What's on your mind, my dear?"

"Something terrible's going on at home."

"Terrible? What d'you mean?"

"Yesterday morning Bubbe suddenly announced that we

need a new mother," she said slowly, playing with a few stray challah crumbs on the table while she tried to steady her voice. "Last night Papa brought a strange man home with him. I didn't like him. He kept *schmoozing* all the time. Bubbe didn't tell me he was coming but she must have known. Papa's so quiet all the time, and… and…" her lips trembled, "I want to know what's going on," she gulped, fighting back her tears.

Auntie Essie gave her a big kiss and hugged her closely. "Don't cry, Becky darling. Come, let's gets warm by the fire." When they were comfortably settled Auntie Essie told her: "Your guest last night was Abe Klein. Everybody knows him, he's a matchmaker."

"A matchmaker? What's that?"

"A matchmaker is a person who arranges marriages."

"He arranges marriages?" Becky repeated. In spite of the heat from the fire, she felt an icy chill trickle slowly down her back.

"Abe's job is to get to know Jewish men and women who want to get married," Auntie Essie explained. "Young and old, poor and not so poor, widows and widowers. When he finds two people who he thinks will suit each other, he introduces them, hoping they will make a good match. That's why he's called a matchmaker, you see."

"Why does Papa need a matchmaker? Why can't he choose someone himself?"

"Don't be foolish, child. He can't just speak to a strange woman without knowing anything about her, or if she comes from a good family. It's just not done. He has to be properly introduced. That's why your father's spoken to Abe Klein."

"Did you and Mama have a matchmaker in Russia?"

"Of course we did. Your father and Uncle Joe were friends of our cousins, which made things easier when the matchmaker introduced us. Our parents gave us their blessing." Auntie Essie smiled. "They say a good marriage is a match made in heaven!"

"Why does Bubbe want Papa to marry again?"

"Bubbe's in a lot of pain with arthritis. You can see how hard it is for her to get up and down stairs. She'd love to go on looking after you and Yossie, but she can't."

"Does he want to get married again?"

"No one can ever replace your mother, that's for sure," Auntie Essie sighed, "but Bubbe's getting worse and your father has to face facts."

There was no holding back now.

"But what about Yossie and me?" Becky sobbed. "Suppose we don't want a new mother, suppose we hate her!"

Auntie Essie cupped Becky's face in her hands and looked into her eyes, which brimmed with tears.

"Becky, darling, don't upset yourself. Your Papa loves you both very much, he wouldn't want to make you unhappy for all the world. You'll just have to trust him."

★ ★ ★

Flat 74 Rothschild Buildings,
Brick Lane,
Whitechapel,
London.

Saturday, 7th November 1908

Dear Mama,

When I got home from Auntie Essie, I was just going upstairs when I heard a door slam and voices. One of them was the strange guest. I hid

14

in a corner of the stairwell so he wouldn't see me. He came downstairs with the lady who sat next to Bubbe in shul this morning. I got a whiff of herrings as she went by. You know I can't stand that smell.

Now – for the Secrets Of My Heart! The strange man is Abe Klein who is a matchmaker. Papa is thinking of getting married again. I am in the depths of despair and my eyes are all red and puffy from crying. Please tell God I don't want that herring smelling lady to be our new mother.

I miss you very much. God bless.

Yours faithfully,

Rebecca Feldman.

Chapter 3

Bubbe muttered to herself as she fumbled in her purse.

"Here Becky," she said, "take this money and get me a few things from Mrs Haffner's shop on your way home from school."

"Why can't I go to Zev's place across the road? Why do I have to *shlep* all the way to a different shop?" Becky asked.

Bubbe ignored her. "Mrs Haffner's shop is just round the corner from Essie and Joe's place. You can't miss it. Be a good girl and write a shopping list for me," she asked, handing her a stub of a pencil and a scrap of paper.

Becky wrote down all the items as Bubbe called them out. The last one was pickled herrings.

"Ugh, herrings! I can't stand the smell! They turn my stomach."

"Nonsense, child!" Bubbe scolded. "Herrings are good

for you and they're cheap. We lived on bread and herrings when things got bad for us Jews in Russia, which was most of the time," she sighed. "Yossie, listen to me. Go to the shop with Becky after school, then she'll take you on to your *cheder* class. Learning Hebrew there is so important."

"Do I have to go?" Yossie sulked.

"Of course you must go. Where else can you learn to read the Torah so one day you'll be a great rabbi?"

"I don't want to be a…"

"Bubbe," Becky interrupted, giving Yossie a 'not now' warning glance. "We're going to be late for school."

"Have you got a towel and soap for the public baths?"

"Its all in my bag," Becky answered, as she kissed her grandmother. "Quick, Yossie. Come on."

Every weekday morning the Rothschild Buildings burst into life with deafening sounds of doors banging, mothers yelling and children shouting to each other as they poured out of their apartments. The moment Becky opened their door they were swept along like a tidal wave with the crowd of children, clattering down the stone steps in a mad dash to get to school on time. Becky suddenly found herself going too fast to stop and collided with a young girl. They landed in a sprawling heap.

"Ouch! Just look what you've done, Yossie!" Becky cried out, clutching her grazed knee and torn stocking.

"It's your fault, you pushed me!"

"I did no such thing! Oh, I could kill you for this," she stormed, trying to pull the edges of the hole together. "My only decent pair of stockings and look at them now – ruined! I'll have to cobble the hole together somehow and I hate darning." She got up and limped over to the girl who was brushing dirt off her skirt.

"I'm sorry," Becky apologised, "I didn't mean to push you

over. I couldn't stop myself in time. Are you okay?"

The girl rubbed her elbow and winced.

"It's nothing much, just a bit sore that's all. I heard you say Yossie. Is he your brother?"

Becky nodded. "Yes, except for the times when I wish he wasn't!" she answered, glaring at him.

"Well, you must be Becky! I was hoping to meet you, though I didn't expect it to be like this," she grinned. "I'm Miriam Lazarus. Everyone calls me Mirrie."

"Where are you living?"

"On the fourth floor. Number 139."

"That's Mrs Kaminsky's isn't it?"

"Yes, she's my great aunt. My mother and I are living with her. D'you know her?"

"Course I do. Everyone knows Mrs Kaminsky. We call her Mrs K. She's very kind, she helped to look after us when my mother died. Are you coming to school? I'll…"

"Becky," Yossie butted in, "before you two start gossiping like old women, I'm going to catch up with the boys."

"Mind your manners and don't be cheeky." She grabbed his hand. "Let's cross the road first. Now listen to me Yossie, don't you dare try riding on the back of those carts or else I'll tell Papa. It's very dangerous. Last week a young boy was nearly killed doing that. Okay? I'll see you later."

"Where's the school?" Mirrie asked as they walked along together.

"Not far now. We go to the bottom of the next street and then it's just around the corner."

Mirrie giggled.

"What's so funny?"

"I met a nice lady on the boat who told me that I would never get lost in this part of the East End of London 'cos everything's 'just around the corner,' the schools, the *shuls,* the shops, the library, the markets. I thought she was joking, but she was right."

"Not quite. She forgot to include the public baths," Becky added. "They're not really 'just round the corner,' but near enough. Oh yes and by the way, it's women's turn on Thursdays and men on Fridays. When did you get here, Mirrie?"

"Last week. I'll never forget that terrible journey as long as I live. The sea was rough, the boat tossed up and down all the time and Mama was so seasick that she thought she was going to die. She's much better now, but she couldn't come with me today. I'm so nervous."

"Why?"

"I'm scared stiff – a new girl in a new school and I don't even speak English very well. My mother's been teaching me, but Yiddish is so much easier, isn't it?"

"Don't worry, you'll learn English very quickly and anyway, most of the teachers can speak some Yiddish. We've taught them!" Becky grinned. "I'll tell you what, I'll ask Miss Bennet if you can be in my class."

"Thanks Becky, I'd like that. What's she like?"

"I think Miss Bennet is the best teacher in the school. She's strict but she's kind, too. I'm trying for a scholarship, so she gives me extra homework. I want to be a teacher as good as she is when I'm grown up."

"Mama keeps telling me that I'll soon make new friends, well I have now, haven't I?" Mirrie asked shyly.

"Course you have! I promise not to knock you down again!"

"Can you come up tonight and meet my mother? She could mend that hole in your stocking quick as anything."

"I'll try. I've got to go shopping after school, then I have to

19

meet my grandmother at the public baths tonight." She thought for a moment. "I'll ask Bubbe if she owes Mrs K a bit of tea or sugar – she usually does. That way I'll have a good excuse to come up."

★ ★ ★

"What's the matter?" Becky asked her brother as they came out of school. "You look very pale. Are you sick or something?"

No answer.

"Is someone bullying you? Come on Yossie, you can tell me y'know."

"I hate Hebrew classes," Yossie cried, "and I hate Rebbe Finegold. He's always pinching us or pulling our ears. I wish I wasn't Jewish, then I wouldn't have to go."

"Don't you dare say things you don't mean. Just think how upset Papa and Bubbe would be if they'd have heard you."

"I don't care," Yossie shouted defiantly. "The gentile boys are so lucky. They don't have to go to cheder to learn Hebrew every day after school except Fridays. They just go home. I even have to go on Sunday mornings as well. It's not fair," he snivelled.

Becky put her arm round his shoulders. "Rebbe Finegold's got no right to pick on you. Papa said that you can read Hebrew really well now. I'll speak to him, okay?"

"I don't want to be a rabbi when I grow up," Yossie whimpered. "I keep telling Bubbe but she won't listen to me."

"Don't cry anymore and I promise you I'll talk to Papa. Look! There's Mrs Haffner's shop. Cheer up and I'll buy you something nice to *nosh*."

The shop was packed with gossiping women and noisy children who got under everyone's feet. Becky couldn't see the counter for the crush. One side of the shop was lined with crates of eggs, sacks of cabbages, carrots, potatoes, flour, sugar, rice, lentils, dried peas, beans, barley and porridge oats. On the other side were rows of wooden barrels brimming with pickled cucumbers, pickled red cabbage, green olives, black olives, and pickled and salted herrings. Becky felt her stomach churn. She swallowed hard. She couldn't help staring at the fish, some packed tightly in layers of coarse salt and some floating in brine, their shiny scales and glassy red eyes gleaming. She looked up. Dangling above her were ropes of onions, garlic and every kind of kosher sausage and salami. The smells were overpowering.

Yossie nudged his sister. "I'm hungry. When is it going to be our turn?"

"Not long now, thank goodness."

They moved nearer to the counter. "Next customer please," the shopkeeper called out.

Becky looked at her and gasped in horror. She was standing face to face with – *the herring lady!*

★ ★ ★

Flat 74 Rothschild Buildings,
Brick Lane,
Whitechapel,
London.

Thursday 12th November 1908

Dear Mama,

Do you remember what you told me about oy vey? Well this is

21

BIG TROUBLE! No wonder Mrs Haffner smells of herrings, she sells them! Bubbe sent Yossie and me to her shop on purpose. She's ugly, she's got a wart on her face with hairs sticking out of it and a wobbly double chin. She humiliated (a Miss Bennet word) me in front of everyone in the shop.

"So these are Jacob Feldman's wonderful children," she shmoozed and went on and on all about us. I was so embarrassed. D'you know what I did? I noticed that one of the wooden barrels of pickled herrings had a loose knot in the wood. I kept on pushing and poking away with my pencil stub until I felt it move. No one saw me. Yossie was too busy eating the biscuits Mrs Haffner gave him. I refused. She wasn't going to bribe me. As we left the shop I saw a trickle of brine leaking from the little hole.

Now – for the Secrets Of My Heart. I am not sorry for what I did. She had it coming.

All my love, God bless.

Yours faithfully,

Rebecca Feldman.

Chapter 4

Becky polished the *Shabbos* candlesticks as if she was in a trance. She had slept badly and her head ached. All because of her terrible dream – more like a nightmare, she thought. It gave her goosebumps every time she thought about it.

She was in Mrs Haffner's shop when she heard a strange creaking noise behind her. She turned around quickly just in time to see a big wooden barrel split in two. It was full of herrings and she watched in horror as they slithered out all over the floor. Mrs Haffner screamed and chased after her. Then, just as she was about to catch her, she slipped and fell. What a sight! Mrs Haffner sprawled on her back and covered in slimy fish! Becky was frantic to escape but she couldn't find Yossie. She looked everywhere until she found him sitting behind the counter eating bagels. They had just reached the shop door when she woke up, cold and trembling.

"You look pale Becky, are you feeling ill?" Bubbe asked. "You were tossing and turning all night. Becky, are you listening to me?"

Becky was startled from her thoughts.

"I'm fine Bubbe," she said quickly, "I was thinking about Mirrie," she lied. "I wish I had shiny black plaits like hers, and dark brown eyes that sparkle when she laughs."

Bubbe frowned. "It's unlucky to talk like that. You mustn't envy someone else, you should thank God there's nothing wrong with your looks. Such a nice little friend you've got, and so quick! Did you see the way she peeled those vegetables? Finished in no time, we were."

She got up slowly and walked to the kitchen. "I must make the challahs and see to the chicken. Hurry up, you'll be late for school. Yossie, come on," she called out. "What are you doing in there?"

★ ★ ★

"What's up, Becky?" Mirrie asked on their way to school. "You sick or something?"

Becky tried to smile. "Bubbe sleeps with me and she kept me awake half the night with her snoring." Another lie. "I'm tired that's all. I'm sorry I couldn't get away yesterday. Thanks for helping us, Bubbe was very pleased."

"Mama keeps telling me that she wants to meet you. Can you come up tomorrow afternoon instead? Your grandmother and your father won't mind will they?"

"No, I don't think so. They usually sleep on *Shabbos* afternoon, so I won't be missed." Becky bit her lip, deep in thought.

"Mirrie, will you do me a favour?"

"Course, I will. What is it?"

Becky coughed and cleared her throat. "I've got to take a message to my Auntie Essie." Yet another lie, *God forgive me*, she said to herself. "Yossie has to meet Papa at the public baths. Can you see he gets there okay?"

"Will he mind coming with me?" Mirrie asked.

"Not if you buy him a bagel. Here's a penny. You can always bribe my little brother with food!"

"Okay. Let's catch him up and I'll tell him to look out for me after school."

★ ★ ★

All day long Becky was haunted by her nightmare. She found it hard to concentrate in class and worst of all, Miss Bennet noticed. "Rebecca can do better," she wrote in her school book. As soon as school was over she ran all the way to Auntie Essie's. She took two steps at a time and arrived breathless outside her door. Delicious smells of baking greeted her before she'd even knocked and walked in. Tonight it was all hustle and bustle; her cousins were helping to prepare for *Shabbos* as if their lives depended on it. Ruth polished the candlesticks and Malka set the table for dinner. Hester, the eldest, was bent over a sewing machine. As soon as she saw Becky, she stopped and rushed over to her.

"Becky, love, what's up? Is Bubbe ill? You look so cold. Here, this'll warm you up," she said, handing her a cup of tea. "Mama!" she shouted. "Guess who's here?"

Auntie Essie stood at the kitchen door and wiped her flushed face with a corner of her apron. She looked at Becky in surprise.

"Becky, dear, what's the matter? Is Bubbe alright?"

"She's fine. I know you're very busy, but…but I've just got to talk to you," she blurted out. "Please, Auntie Essie, it's very important."

Auntie Essie looked at Becky's strained face and nodded. "You'll have to be quick, my dear. You can see how busy we are." She took Becky into the bedroom. "We'll have a bit of peace and quiet in here. Hester," she called over her shoulder, "leave your sewing and carry on with the cooking, there's a good girl. I won't be long."

Becky sat on the bed and told her aunt exactly what she thought about Mrs Haffner. She was careful not to mention the leaking barrel of herrings.

"Is Mrs Haffner the lady who sat next to Bubbe in *shul* last week?" Becky asked.

"Yes."

"Did Bubbe send me and Yossie to her shop so she could meet us?"

Auntie Essie nodded.

"She…she can't be the lady Abe Klein wants Papa to marry, can she? Please, oh please tell me she isn't." Scalding, salty tears splashed down her face. Auntie Essie stroked her hair.

"Becky don't cry. Listen to me. I know it's hard for you, but you must try to understand. Mrs Haffner will make a good match for your papa. She's hard-working and a good business woman. It's only a small shop but she makes a good living."

"Well, so does Papa when he's on overtime," Becky answered defiantly. "He's a master craftsman. The foreman at the workshop said so."

Auntie Essie rolled her eyes and sighed.

"He may as well be the finest cabinet maker in the whole wide world," she said, "but what good's that when there's no work? Have you forgotten what happened during the strike?"

Becky blew her nose. Auntie Essie was right, of course. She would never ever forget how ashamed she felt having to stand in line at the Jewish charity soup kitchen. Even worse was the fear of being evicted if they couldn't pay the rent. They pawned everything they could, but they were always cold and hungry. Yossie was all skin and bone and Mama used to pretend she wasn't hungry and gave him her food. She sniffed, wiped her eyes and forced herself to ask the next question. She dreaded the answer.

"Are they going to get married?"

Auntie Essie shrugged. "Your father's thinking about it."

"But she smells of herrings!"

Auntie Essie tried hard not to smile.

"Honestly, Becky, the things you come out with! Doesn't your father reek of the horse-hoof glue he uses in the workshop? I'm sure I smell of fried fish right now. So what? The public baths are just round the corner!"

"I don't want Mrs Haffner to be our stepmother!" Becky shouted. "She could never ever be like Mama and I…hate her!"

"Becky how can you say such a thing? Why you've only met her once, and that was in her busy shop. Be fair now and give the poor woman a chance. Ever since her husband died she's had to run the shop almost single-handed, as well as looking after her children. You'll have new sisters and brothers, it'll be good company for you." She stood up and opened the door.

"Now you'd best be getting home or Bubbe'll start to worry. I've got to finish the cooking before your Uncle Joe and the boys get home from *shul*. Don't upset yourself, Becky, everything will turn out for the best, you'll see. Give my love to everyone. Good *Shabbos*."

"I feel so sorry for that poor kid," Hester said when Becky

had left. "She's not going to take kindly to a stepmother is she?"

"No, she's not. Becky was very close to her mother," Auntie Essie sighed.

"What about Uncle Jacob?"

"Becky told me that he makes excuses whenever she tries to talk to him. I can understand why. Jacob is a shy man and it's not the kind of thing he can discuss with a child. It's too personal. He's worried about Bubbe and the children and I don't think he knows what to do for the best."

"D'you think he'll get married again?"

"Your guess is as good as mine, Hester. I think it's the only sensible solution and I pray to God that Becky is old enough to realise that. Mrs Haffner is a good, God-fearing woman, I'm sure she'll be good to her and Yossie."

"You'll have a hard time convincing Becky about that."

"I know, I know. Becky is such a headstrong child. I only hope that she doesn't cause any trouble and go and upset Mrs Haffner."

★ ★ ★

Flat 74 Rothschild Buildings,
Brick Lane,
Whitechapel,
London.

Friday 13th November 1908

Dear Mama,

Bubbe lost the rent book – again! She had the five shillings ready on the dresser, but she couldn't find the book. She gets into such a state.

28

"Oy vey! Oy vey!" she kept moaning. *"The superintendent'll be here soon and if we can't pay the rent he'll throw us out into the street."* We had to drop everything and turn the place upside down, until finally Yossie found it underneath the dresser. Next time, we'll look there first!

I've got a lovely new friend called Mirrie Lazarus. She's good company and very kind and gave me a pair of her old stockings which are too small for her.

I've been thinking that if Papa marries You Know Who, we'll have to live with all those awful Haffner kids. The eldest boy, Sol, is a big bully. No one likes him at school. I'll have to work in the shop with the Haffner girls. That means there'll be no chance of me trying for a scholarship. I'm getting goosebumps all the time these days.

Now – for the Secrets Of My Heart. I get so angry when Papa or Bubbe keep on saying 'no buts' every time I ask a question. You never did, and neither does Auntie Essie. Papa thinks that what's going on doesn't concern me. He's wrong because it does, it really does. I'll soon be eleven and I'm old enough to understand. I just hate not knowing.

Goodnight and God bless.

Yours faithfully,

Rebecca Feldman.

Chapter 5

'Your father is thinking about it,' Auntie Essie had told her. Becky was too, until her head ached.

As soon as Meg had left with a whispered "Good *Shabbos*," Becky remembered something Miss Bennet never tired of telling them. "Now girls, don't be scatterbrains. You must learn to think clearly." Becky told herself sternly that that's just what she must do. She pressed her hands on each side of her head so she could concentrate really hard.

First of all Papa hadn't made up his mind yet, which was not exactly good news, but something to hold on to. But how long would it be before he did, she asked herself: a week, a month, a year? Next, as long as there was still time she would keep on trying to make papa see that he would be making a terrible mistake if he married Mrs H. *I've got no one to help me so I'll have to fight this battle alone,* she muttered to herself with clenched teeth. From now on she would watch and wait. That, she nodded thoughtfully, was something she could do.

Mrs Haffner wasn't in *shul,* and when Becky looked down where Papa and Yossie were sitting, she couldn't see Abe Klein either. Maybe he was busy looking for another man to introduce to Mrs Herring. *Please God help him to find someone soon*, she prayed.

Mirrie nudged her.

"Stop daydreaming, Becky. Don't forget, Mama's expecting you this afternoon," she whispered.

"D'you think she'll like me?"

"Course, she will, silly. She's really looking forward to meeting my best friend! Mama has gone to help our next door neighbour who slipped and fell this morning, so I've got to collect the cholent."

"Good! I'll get ours as well. We can go together after the service." Becky told her quietly.

It was a cold raw day. Horses snorted clouds of steam and sent sparks flying from their hoofs as they clattered along the shiny cobblestones. Once inside the warm bakehouse, the girls waited their turn, breathing in the mouth-watering smells of savoury stews. Mr Marston called out the tag numbers as he pulled them out of the oven one by one. Slowly and carefully, the girls carried their pots home. They stopped outside Becky's door.

"Mmmm! Your cholent smells good," Becky sniffed. "What's in it?"

"Just the usual, a bit of meat, carrots, potatoes and dumplings."

"Dumplings are Papa's favourites. Bubbe hasn't made them for ages."

"My mouth's watering, I'm starving," Mirrie gulped,

wiping her mouth with the back of her hand. "I hope Mama's home by now, because if she isn't then I'm going to help myself! See you later."

Becky knew that a plateful of hot, tasty cholent with lots of gravy never failed to put her father in a good mood. As soon as they had finished eating she asked nervously, "Can I go upstairs now to see Mirrie?"

"Mirrie?" Papa asked.

"She's my new friend. She lives upstairs with her mother and Mrs K. She's very nice, isn't she Bubbe?"

Bubbe nodded. "What a lovely girl! She's got a good head on her shoulders that one and good company for our Becky."

Papa wiped his mouth and pushed back his chair.

"We've got a *Shabbos* guest coming this afternoon. Tidy yourself up a bit Becky and make Yossie look presentable."

"What's her name?"

"Mrs Haffner."

"But…!"

"No buts Becky," Papa snapped, opening his prayer book.

The shock of Papa's sudden announcement made her feel angry and sick. *Why was that woman coming again? Why hadn't Bubbe told Papa that Yossie and I went to see her in the shop? Oh God, I've got to get out of this somehow*, she seethed inside herself.

"Go and rest now, Mama, Becky'll clear up." Becky's father said.

"Papa, Yossie and I have already…"

"Call me in an hour." He picked up the newspaper and went into his bedroom.

"Is that the lady who gave me a bag of biscuits?" Yossie asked.

"Yes, and I'm not going to sit with her all afternoon," Becky hissed defiantly. "I've got a plan. Help me clear away these plates, I'll wash them up later. Don't argue, don't make a noise and don't tell Bubbe you've been helping me, otherwise she'll tell me off for giving you 'woman's work'. Come on."

When the dishes were piled up in the kitchen, Yossie washed his hands and face and Becky combed his hair.

"That's better," she said, rubbing some stains off his jacket. "Yossie, will you do me a big favour?"

Yossie was watching a cockroach scuttle across the floor. "What's it worth?" he asked, crushing the insect with his foot.

"I'll buy you a cinnamon bun after school on Monday?"

No answer. Becky was getting desperate.

"*If* I have enough money, I'll buy you a cinnamon bun and two bagels, alright?"

"Okay. What d'you want?"

"Go upstairs to Mrs K's place, number 139 on the fourth floor. Tell Mirrie we've got a guest this afternoon and ask her to come and get me at four o'clock. I'm sure Papa won't refuse me. Then I want you to listen to everything that's going on while I'm upstairs, so you can tell me when I get back."

"That's crazy Becky; how can I remember everything they talk about?"

"Just do it, Yossie. For God's sake, just try and do it for me!" Becky hissed, close to tears.

"Alright, okay, I'll do it, I'll do it. Calm down," he said quickly. Becky opened the door quietly.

"Now don't forget," she whispered. "Tell Mirrie to call for me at four o'clock. Don't tell Bubbe and Papa where you've been. If they ask you, just keep quiet – keep *schtum*, okay?"

Yossie nodded and disappeared upstairs.

Becky flopped down on a chair near the fire. The wind was howling down the chimney. She gathered her skirt round her ankles and pulled her knees up to her chin. "It's not fair," she muttered to herself. "It's just not fair. Auntie Essie thinks Mrs H will be a good match and I'm sure Bubbe does too. What about Papa? He doesn't look as if he does and he doesn't look happy either. He's been in a funny, grumpy mood all day."

She was so deep in thought she didn't hear Yossie return. "Well?"

"It's fine," Yossie grinned. "Mirrie'll be here at four o'clock."

"Thanks Yossie. I've got to get washed now."

★ ★ ★

The best cups and saucers were set out on the table. Yossie hovered round the plate of cakes. Bubbe smoothed down her dress and fussed with her head scarf. Papa wore his one good jacket and looked nervous. Becky watched the clock.

"Good *Shabbos,* good *Shabbos,*" Mrs Haffner smiled when she arrived. She wore a black felt hat and her shiny black dress smelt of moth balls. She had several gold rings sunk deep into her fleshy fingers. "Here's a little something for your supper, Mrs Feldman," she smiled, handing Bubbe a small parcel.

Bubbe unwrapped a few slices of smoked salmon – a rare treat. "Thank you, you're very kind. There's nothing my son enjoys more, isn't that right, Jacob?"

Papa fidgeted in his chair. He nodded and smiled. Mrs Haffner beckoned to Yossie.

"Come here, child," she ordered. "Did you like my shop?" she asked, pinching his cheek.

"Ouch!...Yes I did. Oh, thanks for the biscuits," he said, rubbing his face.

"Such a polite little boy! Come in any time, Yossie, dear, I'll give you some bagels and pretzels."

Becky clenched her fists in anger. How dare she bribe Yossie. She wasn't going to buy Becky off with gifts of food.

"My customers got a real bargain yesterday," Mrs Haffner boasted. "I had to sell off a whole barrel of pickled herrings at less than half price. To be honest, I was more or less giving them away."

Becky felt her cheeks burning. She didn't know where to look. She turned round and fussed with the plates on the dresser so that nobody could see her red face.

"Why was that?" Bubbe asked.

"One of those knots of wood in the barrel must have worked loose, and all the brine leaked out. *Oy vey!* What a mess! I had to get my two eldest girls to help me clear up. We didn't finish till late. I had no choice but to sell the herrings off quickly."

Becky went into the kitchen. She was so angry with Mrs Haffner. Why did she have to tell Papa and Bubbe? Thank God she didn't know it was her. She opened a cupboard door and accidentally knocked over a box of vegetables, which crashed to the floor.

"Are you alright, Becky? What's happening in there?" Bubbe called.

"Nothing, nothing. I dropped something, that's all."

Just then there was a knock on the door. Becky grabbed a large onion. An idea flashed into her mind.

Papa opened the door.

"Good *Shabbos*. I'm Mirrie."

"Come in, come in."

"My mother sent these for you, Mrs Feldman." She put a plate of homemade biscuits on the table. "Can Becky come and have tea with us?" Mirrie asked, smiling at everyone.

"Thank you, my dear," Bubbe smiled. "Yes, of course she can. I forgot to tell you, Jacob. I sent the children to Mrs Haffner's shop on…"

"Papa, Yossie and I have already met Mrs Haffner," Becky interrupted hurriedly. She gave Yossie a warning look, grabbed Mirrie's hand and pulled her out of the door.

★ ★ ★

"Well, well, so we meet at last! Mirrie hasn't stopped talking about you since you bumped into each other!" Mrs Lazarus smiled. She looked closely at Becky's tense, pale face.

"Come and sit down by the fire, Becky. You look as if you could do with a nice hot drink, yes?"

A cup of tea and a slice of cake soon revived her spirits. "It's ages since I was here. It's all so different, so cosy," Becky said, looking around the room. The walls were freshly whitewashed. There was a bright coloured cloth on the table and a new curtain across the bed-alcove. The shelves above the dresser were edged with a paper frill and a row of cups hung from the bottom shelf.

"I'm glad you like it. Mrs K, as you call her, is pleased too."

"Where is she?" Becky asked.

"She had to go all the way to Liverpool early yesterday morning. Her brother, my uncle, is very ill. He lives on his own so my aunt went to nurse him."

"Where's that?" Becky asked, looking at a framed picture of a village scene.

"That's Pochep in Russia, where we used to live."

"Who are those men in the photograph?"

"This one," Mrs Lazarus explained, pointing to the young man, "Is my late husband. He and his friend Hershel went to America together to start a new life. He was going to send for us to join him, but sadly he died in an accident. Hershel is such a good man," she said with a far away look in her eyes. "He really cares about me, you know, and writes to me regularly. That's my late father. He was a bookseller and a fine Jewish scholar. He taught me to read and write Hebrew, Yiddish and English too. Does that surprise you, Becky?" she asked.

Becky nodded and helped herself to more cake.

"Young Jewish girls had to help at home until they got married. They had no education at all," Mrs Lazarus explained. "The boys were lucky. They were taught in religious schools." She got up to make more tea. "Here I go rattling on. I'm sure you must be getting bored."

"I'm not. Please go on," Becky pleaded.

"My father and I used to love riding in the wagon to the country fairs. We rented a stall in the market place, unpacked the books and waited for customers. What crowds there were! Grain merchants, matchmakers, second-hand clothes dealers, rag-sorters and peasants shopping for bargains. Those good times have gone forever," Mrs Lazarus nodded sadly. "All we hear of these days are terrible stories about pogroms when Russian soldiers, without any cause or warning, would ride into little towns and villages to burn down synagogues and kill innocent Jewish people. We're very, very lucky to live in a free country with a roof over our heads. Mirrie's very lucky to have such a good friend. Thank you for helping her to settle down in school, that means a lot to both of us."

★ ★ ★

Flat 74 Rothschild Buildings,
Brick Lane,
Whitechapel,
London.

Saturday 14th November 1908

Dear Mama,

Mrs Haffner came for tea. She didn't stop talking about the leaking herring barrel so I got my revenge! When no one was looking – guess what I did – I dropped an onion in the samovar!! You would have been so proud of Yossie. He remembered to tell me everything that happened when I went upstairs to see Mirrie's mother. As soon as Mrs Haffner drank her tea, she made a terrible face and spat it all out! "Ugh!" she shuddered, "it tastes of onion!" Poor Bubbe made her another cup which tasted exactly the same! To make things worse the chimney started to smoke. That wasn't my fault, though I bet I'll get blamed for it. Yossie said he nearly got the giggles watching Mrs Haffner spluttering over her tea, coughing and choking on the smoke and frantically brushing bits of soot off her dress.

In the middle of all this someone came with an urgent message for Papa. Yossie didn't know who he was, but I guess someone wanted Papa to read or translate a letter. Anyway, Papa excused himself and went off with the man. I bet he was glad of the chance to escape. Mrs Haffner left soon after – in a huff, Yossie said.

Now – for the Secrets Of My Heart. I hope Mrs H has got my message – she's not, I repeat, not welcome here!
God bless.

Yours faithfully,

Rebecca Feldman.

Chapter 6

Bubbe grunted in her sleep. Becky opened her eyes and looked at the damp patches on the ceiling. Each one seemed to take on a different shape: a galloping horse, a huge elephant and a tall tree in the far corner. What was the one above the door? Was she imagining things or did it look just like Mrs Haffner's hat? She shivered and looked away.

The room was so cold that her warm breath made little clouds of steam. During the night the inside of the window had iced over in a pretty snowflake pattern. She heard Papa making the fire in the living room. I'm in for it now, she thought, clutching her churning stomach. She slid quietly out of bed and dressed quickly, her teeth chattering with the cold.

Papa was angry. She could tell by the hunch of his shoulders and the way he rattled the poker in the grate.

"Thank goodness the wind has dropped and the chimney's

stopped smoking." Becky tried to sound cheerful. "Don't worry, Papa, I'll clear up all the mess."

Papa turned round quickly, still clutching the poker.

"What's got into you lately, Becky?" he shouted. "I thought you were a responsible young girl. Yesterday you behaved like a very silly child. You upset our *Shabbos* guest and you made me feel ashamed."

Becky felt her eyes sting and her lips trembled. Papa put the poker down and threw another lump of coal on the fire. He brushed the dirt off his hands and took his jacket off the hook.

"Becky, are you listening to me?"

She nodded without looking up.

"Let this be an end to your stupid, crazy pranks, d'you hear me?"

Becky nodded again.

"One thing's for sure," he said, as he opened the door, "you really do need a new mother. Someone who can talk a bit of sense into you," he snapped, slamming the door behind him.

Becky sobbed until her head throbbed. Her father's words 'you made me feel ashamed,' pierced her like a stab in the heart. Everything had gone terribly wrong. She thought the onion-flavoured tea might have put Mrs Haffner off and stopped the match. Instead it had done just the opposite. She had made her father angry and pushed him nearer than ever to getting married.

"*Oy vey! Oy vey!*" Bubbe winced, as she hobbled into the room. "The damp weather's no good for my legs."

Becky wiped her eyes quickly. She didn't want Bubbe to see she'd been crying. She took the kettle off the iron ring above the fire and carefully poured the boiling water into the teapot. Then she cut a slice of bread, speared it on the long handled fork, and toasted it over the fire, first one side, then the other.

"Here, Bubbe, this'll make you feel better," she said.

"Thank you, dear," Bubbe said, crunching her toast. "There was such a funny taste to the tea, yesterday. Your father had to wash out the samovar several times last night to get rid of it."

Becky kept very quiet. *Perhaps she doesn't know that I did it – yet!*

"Yossie dear," Bubbe said when the boy appeared. "I forgot to tell you I had a message from your Uncle Joe. He's just finished a tailoring job and he's got enough cloth left over to make you a pair of trousers. God knows, you need them," she sighed, looking at his shabby pair. "He wants you to go round there after cheder. Becky'll go with you."

Later, Becky walked with Yossie as far as the entrance to Auntie Essie's building. "I haven't got time to come up with you, Yossie. Tell them I've got to help Bubbe." It wasn't much of an excuse, but it saved her from having to face the family. *They'll hear all about the onion tea soon enough, and I know whose side Auntie Essie'll be on*, she thought bitterly.

The flat was empty when she got back. There was such a strong smell of damp soot it made her nostrils curl. She stood in the middle of the room and shouted defiantly at the four walls.

"I'll show you, Papa, I'll show you that I AM RESPONSIBLE!" With that, she rolled up her sleeves and set to work. She put more coal on the fire, swept up the soot from the hearth, washed the floor, scrubbed the table, and was dusting the furniture when Yossie returned.

"Get your shoes off!" Becky ordered. "Don't you dare

dirty my nice clean floor! Just look at you! Have you been playing in the yard?"

"So what?"

"Papa told you not to, that's what. It's like a sheet of ice down there. Where's your new trousers?"

"They're not finished. Hester'll bring them when we meet her in the market tonight. Anything to eat, Becky? I'm starving."

"There's some challah left," Becky called out from the kitchen. "I'll heat up the soup when Bubbe gets back."

"Where's she gone?"

"To see Mrs Sokolov, I think."

"What you doing?" Yossie asked, chewing a crust.

"What does it look like?" Becky replied, sorting dirty clothes into piles.

"You're not doing the washing now, are you? I hate it when the whole place gets full of steam. It makes me choke. Can't you leave it till tomorrow?"

"I don't have much time to help on a Monday," Becky said, tossing some shirts into the copper boiler, "and it's a lot of work for Bubbe to do on her own. This'll be a nice surprise for her." *Papa too, I hope*, she said to herself.

"Damn! The tap's got stuck again," Becky growled, gritting her teeth with the effort. "It's got so rusty, it just won't turn."

"Papa said we need a new one," Yossie mumbled with his mouth full.

"Well that's not much help to me now, is it?" Becky shouted angrily. She tried again. "Come on, come on, move, move, you damn stupid thing!" This time she wrenched it so hard it broke off with a loud snap. She stood there, horrified, still clutching the tap as water poured down the wall behind the sink.

"Oh, God! Quick, Yossie, grab some towels, cloths, anything! Here, hold this over the pipe, else we'll be flooded!" Becky shouted, trying desperately to stop the flow of water.

"What we going to do? *Oy vey*! My feet are getting wet."

A loud hammering on the door made them both jump. It was Mr Harris from the flat below.

"What the hell's going on in here? There's water coming through our ceiling!"

"The tap broke off in my hand," Becky cried.

"Alright, calm down, Becky. I know where the stopcock is. Out of my way!" He bent down and fumbled behind the boiler.

"That's it – all done! I've turned the water off. Look! See? It's stopped. You'll soon get dried out."

"Thanks very much, Mr Harris," Becky snivelled.

He turned the tap over in his hands.

"I'm afraid it's too far gone to repair." He looked up.

"Oh, there you are, Jacob. I was just telling Becky you'll have to buy a new tap. Look here. D'you see? The thread has worn quite thin."

Papa was speechless! The little kitchen was in chaos: dirty washing strewn everywhere, dripping cloths wrapped around the broken pipe, the children on their hands and knees mopping the wet floor.

"It was an accident, Jacob," Mr Harris explained. "I've turned the water off, so there's no need to panic."

Papa managed to find his voice.

"Thanks Oscar, is your ceiling damaged?" he asked.

"Nothing that a coat of whitewash won't put right. It'll have to wait for warmer weather. By the way, I saw Abe Klein in the building yesterday. Did he come and see you?"

Papa looked embarrassed. He nodded.

"I thought so. I'm glad you've come to your senses at last, Jacob. I hope Abe finds you a good match. It's hard enough for your mother, I know, and Becky's a great help, but she's only a child. You need to marry again, Jacob, and the sooner the better."

★ ★ ★

"Hester told me she's going to buy us a toffee apple," Yossie chatted on their way to the market.

No reply.

"Are you in a bad mood, Becky?"

"What's it look like?"

"It wasn't your fault, y'know."

"Oh yeah? Who says so?"

"Bubbe."

"How d'you know?"

Yossie cleared his throat and mimicked Bubbe's voice: "Jacob, how many times have I asked you to fix that tap? You mustn't blame Becky, she was only trying to help me."

Becky smiled. "Bubbe really said that, honestly?"

"Honestly," Yossie grinned. "And…"

"And what?"

"From now on, no more steamy kitchen!"

"What d'you mean?"

"Mrs Harris has got us a washerwoman who's going to collect our dirty clothes every week. I can't remember how much it'll cost. Cheer up, Becky, I hate it when you've got a long face on you."

"Thanks Yossie. You're a good kid – sometimes!"

Becky loved the market on a dark, winter's afternoon. Hissing naphtha torches lit up the stalls and the strange light seemed to give everyone a yellow-greenish complexion. They stopped to watch a couple of buskers. One of them played a tin whistle whilst the other sang and danced.

"Look, she's over there!"

Hester, clutching her parcels and two toffee apples, waved to them from the china stall.

"Come on, now, ladies!" the man shouted, tossing china plates in the air and catching them. "Only six pennies! You won't get a better bargain anywhere else. Why, I'm almost giving them away!"

"How does he manage to throw all those plates in the air and catch them without breaking any?" Becky stood watching, fascinated.

"Practice, I think," Hester said. "It must be good for business 'cause there's always a big crowd here. Yossie, can you see the organ grinder over there? Here's some peanuts for his little monkey. Watch out he doesn't snatch your toffee apple! We'll wait here for you." She gave Becky two parcels. "Here's Yossie's trousers, and this one is for you."

"For me? Really? Thank you very much," Becky said, grinning with excitement as she unwrapped the paper and held up a dark blue wool dress.

"Oh, Hester it's lovely and the collar's so pretty."

"Round collars are all the fashion now. I made it out of a bit of shiny coat lining which I pinched from the factory," she grinned. "The dress is only a hand-me-down y'know, but there's plenty of wear left in it. I've put three tucks in the skirt. Let's see," she said, measuring it up against Becky. "That's good, it's just the right length."

"I'm going to keep it for best and wear it for *shul.*"

Hester put her arm round Becky's shoulder. "Listen to me, Becky love. I know things are hard for you right now, but if your father decides to marry Mrs Haffner, there's no use fighting against it. You'll just have to make the best of it."

"Well, I'm not going to make the best of it. If he marries that awful woman, I'm going to run away!"

"Oh yeah! Where to, us? We're already three in a bed! Don't talk like a silly kid. Whatever happens in a family, you just have to put up with it. You're not the only one, you know," Hester sighed.

"What d'you mean?"

"I hate working in the factory making buttonholes all day long, it's back aching and boring. I want to work in the West End of London and sew smart clothes for rich ladies. I'd give anything to get some training in fashion design."

"Why can't you? You're so clever with the needle."

"Training costs a lot of money and my wages are needed at home. It's as simple as that. One day I hope we might be able to afford it, but we can't now. I just have to make the best of it – see what I mean? Here's Yossie." Hester gave Becky a hug and a kiss. "You're a brave kid Becky. Things'll work out, you'll see."

★ ★ ★

Flat 74 Rothschild Buildings,
Brick Lane,
Whitechapel,
London.

Sunday 15th November 1908

Dear Mama,

Mrs Reitzner has just had another baby – number six! Where's she going to put it? The last one slept in a drawer! I know Bubbe will send me up there with some cake or something and Mrs R will beg me to stay and look after the others. I absolutely HATE that. They're dirty and smelly and they all have runny noses. It makes me want to throw up. I don't want to go, but I know you would tell me it would be a mitzvah – my good deed, so I guess I'll go after I've done my homework. That'll please you.

It's very cold and damp here. Bubbe says at least we should be thankful that the milk doesn't go sour like it does in the hot summer. The bed bugs must feel the cold too, they don't bite so hard in the winter time!

Now – for the Secrets Of My Heart. Mr Harris saw Abe Klein when he came to see Papa. He's told Mrs Harris and, well – like you used to say: "Whoosh! Rumour spreads through this building as fast as a forest fire!" Nothing's happened yet, but I'm going to fight against the marriage with the last ounce of breath in my body. I know that sounds dramatic, but it's how I feel.

All my love, God bless.

Yours faithfully,

Rebecca Feldman

Chapter 7

Bubbe's face was all crumpled with pain.

"I'm not going to the public baths this afternoon," she said, sucking in her breath with each attack. "I'll have a good wash in front of the fire."

"You'll be all on your own," Becky said anxiously. "Mrs K's gone to Liverpool. Shall I ask Mrs Sokolov to pop in?"

"Don't worry, child, I can manage. The pain comes and goes, first in my legs, then in my knees," she sighed. "Now what was I going to ask you? Oh, yes. Take that to your father," she said, pointing to a basket on the table. "That'll tide him over 'till he gets home. He's got a rush job on and he'll be late tonight. Have you got your towel and clean underwear ready? And soap?"

"I'll get some." Becky dashed into the kitchen.

"Becky dear," Bubbe called out to her.

"Here it comes," Becky muttered under her breath. "She's going to tell me not to waste the soap!" She put her hand over her mouth to stop herself giggling.

"Did you hear me Becky? Don't leave the soap in the bath water, it's so wasteful and expensive."

★ ★ ★

The foreman of the carpenter's workshop was covered from head to foot in sawdust. His cap, his apron, his beard, his moustache, and even his eyebrows. *He looks just as if he's been caught in a snowstorm*, Becky thought.

"You Jacob's girl?"

Becky nodded.

"I bet there's something good to eat in that basket, lucky man. You'd best take it to him, then," he said. "You know where he is?"

Becky nodded again and stepped into the warm workshop. The air was filled with strong odours of wood, resin, sawdust and sweat. She passed rows of newly finished chairs, tables and cupboards. Some had been made from oak, the rest mahogany and walnut, all waiting for a coat of varnish.

The screeching of the great cutting machines was deafening. A short flight of steps in the far corner led up to another quieter workshop. The cabinet makers were busy sawing, planing, and sandpapering. A pot of horse-hoof glue bubbled away on a small gas ring and the stench made Becky want to throw up. Papa was bent over his workbench, pushing his jackplane forwards and backwards along a thick plank of wood. She stood fascinated, watching the smooth wood shavings fly up in perfect curls and cascade on to the floor. Just then he looked up and smiled. *A good sign*, Becky thought.

"Bubbe sent some soup and sandwiches," she said, holding up the basket. Papa carefully placed his tools in a rack on the wall, then he wiped his hands on his apron, releasing a cloud of sawdust.

"Come over here," he said, pointing to a rough bench against the wall. He peered into the basket and lifted out an enamel can with a cup-shaped lid. It was filled with cold beetroot soup.

"Want some *borscht*?" Papa asked, pouring the soup into the cup. "There's plenty here."

"No thanks."

He broke off a chunk of his pickled beef sandwich for Becky and took a large bite for himself. She hated seeing his knuckles all swollen with corns, they looked so painful. 'A cabinet maker's trademark,' Papa always called them. When he had finished eating, he took out a packet of cigarette papers and a tin of tobacco. He sprinkled the tobacco on to one of the cigarette papers. Slowly and carefully he rolled it up, licked the glued edge and stuck it down and lit it. Becky was waiting. If he blew smoke rings for her, it would mean he wasn't angry any more. He inhaled deeply, threw back his head, and opened his mouth wide in the shape of an 'O'. One by one, he blew perfect smoke rings into the air.

"So, how's school? Are you still top in English?"

"Yes," she answered shyly. "Miss Bennet gives me lots of homework. She wants me to try for a scholarship next year."

"How's Bubbe?"

"She's not coming to the public baths."

"Why not?" Papa sounded worried. "What's wrong?"

"She's got pains in her legs again. I'll help her as soon as I get back."

"What d'you think of this, Becky?" Papa asked, reaching

51

behind his workbench and holding up a small carved shelf. "Best quality mahogany. I had a piece left over."

"It's beautiful, Papa, thank you." Becky beamed with pleasure. She stroked the wood and trailed her fingers along the fine fretwork patterns which decorated the edge. "It'll be perfect for my Russian nesting dolls."

"It'll look quite different when it's French polished. There's too much sawdust flying around in here for that. Moishe said he'll do it for me." He put the shelf back, took his tools from the rack and carefully stubbed out his cigarette butt with his foot.

"Papa, I…I want to…"

"Not now, not now," he said hurriedly, "I'm too busy. I've got to get back to work." He felt in his pocket and took out a penny. He pressed it in her hand and kissed the top of her head. "Everything will work out for the best, Becky," he muttered. "But remember, don't meddle in grown up affairs."

★ ★ ★

The cold wind whipped Becky's skirt round her legs and tugged at her basket, but she hardly noticed. Papa had forgiven her for all the trouble last week. Why else would he make her such a beautiful shelf? She was so happy that she could have danced in the street. She ran all the way to the public baths and arrived out of breath, her cheeks glowing. Inside, the hot steamy atmosphere was drenched in a strong smell of disinfectant and carbolic soap. And what a noise! Doors banging, people shouting, children yelling, freshly scrubbed women and girls chatting to each other on their way out. Becky sat on a wooden bench and waited her turn for a bath. Mrs Levy, the bath attendant, looked hot and flustered. No wonder; it was her job to provide hot water for each bath. This was supplied from a tap outside each numbered cubicle. The bathers drove her mad.

"Hot water in number four."

"More hot water in number eleven, please."

"Are you there, Mrs Levy? Hot water in number three."

"I'm freezing in here, Mrs Levy! Where are you? Hot water in number seventeen. Hurry up!"

"I'm coming, I'm coming already!" Mrs Levy shouted above the noise. "Have a little mercy! I've only got one pair of hands, I can't be everywhere at once," she grumbled, mopping the sweat off her face.

"Is your Bubbe not well again?" she asked Becky, as she lead the way into cubicle number nine. "Tell her I've got something for her arthritis." She turned on the cold water with a tap key and cleaned the bath with a long-handled brush dipped in disinfectant.

"Remember, your time's up in half an hour," Mrs Levy warned, as she took Becky's money and closed the door behind her.

Becky stood waiting until the hot water filled the bath, belching clouds of steam. She undressed, grabbed her soap and stepped into the bath. It was ages since she had had a bath all to herself. She wallowed and splashed happily, half listening to snatches of conversation that floated in and out of the cubicles.

"Fanny can you hear me? D'you know my cousin Gittle told me that Abe Klein is wearing out his boot leather trying to fix up a good match for Sadie?"

Becky sat bolt upright so fast that she almost lost her balance. The soap shot out of her hand and plopped into the water. She was sure Mrs Haffner's name was Sadie. She sat very still, straining every muscle to listen to the rest of the gossip.

"Well, I suppose she can afford to be picky. Her husband left her well provided and she makes a good living from the shop…"

"Number six, more hot water, please."

Becky groaned with frustration. "Go on, go on, please go on. Don't stop talking," she whispered to herself. She waited for what seemed an age before she heard the women's voices again.

"Fanny, are you there?"

"Yes, I'm here. What were you saying?"

"I said, God help the man Sadie finally chooses. He'll have to work like a donkey."

"I heard that her husband, God rest his soul, was very strict with the kids."

"Y'don't say!"

"Oh yes, it's well known that he would lay into the boys with his belt."

"Well, it's a different story now. Sadie spoils 'em rotten, and they've got a bit wild. Gittle says the older girls work like slaves." The voices were interrupted by a hammering on a door.

"Hey! Can you hear me in number fifteen. Your time's up," Mrs Levy shouted.

The gossips continued.

"Sadie's not much of a cook, y'know. I suppose she's too busy in the shop. D'you know what Gittle told me?"

Becky shivered. The bath water was getting cold. She didn't dare ask for more hot water for fear of missing anything.

"Gittle was invited to *Shabbos* dinner last week. You'll never guess what she told me. She could hardly eat the cholent; the meat was as tough as old boot leather and the gravy was all dried up!"

Just then, Mrs Levy banged on the door, making Becky jump.

"Number nine, your time's up!" she shouted. Then, without warning, the bath water drained away. It was as if an invisible hand had pulled out the plug. Becky had no choice but to rescue the slimy soap, dry herself quickly and get dressed.

There was an icy wind outside. Becky wrapped her shawl closer round her neck and clutched at her headscarf. The lamplighter was busy with his long pole lighting the gas lamps, which cast little pools of light as he went down the street. Becky's mind was reeling. What she had overheard in the public baths would change everything. Mrs Haffner is a bad cook. *Papa won't want to marry her now*, Becky thought. He just couldn't, not after all of her mama's delicious meals. She must find a way of warning him, but how? Would he believe her? Would that really change his mind? There was no doubt about it. In spite of Papa's warning, she was going to have to MEDDLE AGAIN!

★ ★ ★

Flat 74 Rothschild Buildings,
Brick Lane,
Whitechapel,
London.

Thursday 19th November 1908

Dear Mama,

Very sad news; Mrs Reitzner's baby died. Everyone said that she was a sickly little thing from the moment she was born. The neighbours are helping out by taking it in turns to have the children until Mrs R feels better. The two older girls were here yesterday. Bubbe gave me some clean rags so I cleaned them up a bit and then we played with your button box. It kept them quiet for ages!

Now – for the Secrets Of My Heart. I've heard some very important gossip. Mrs H can't make a decent cholent. I've got to tell Papa. If nothing else will change his mind, surely this will. Please tell God to be on my side.

God bless you, Mama.

Yours faithfully,

Rebecca Feldman.

Chapter 8

"Becky, can we get some bagels?" Yossie asked when they came out of school. "I'm starving!"

"You're always starving. I've got no money."

"I have," Yossie boasted.

"We'll have to be quick then, Bubbe'll go mad if I'm not home soon. Come on, Mirrie."

Becky guided her brother carefully over the steaming horse dung, squashed cabbage leaves and rotting vegetables which littered the market place. The bagel woman was sitting on a wooden box in between two stalls. She wore an old patched coat tied with string, a moth-eaten grey shawl round her shoulders and a man's flat cap on her head. Next to her was a large sack bulging with bagels.

"Bagels, hot bagels!" the woman croaked. She grinned at the children, showing her bright pink gums, bare except for the one single tooth. She took Yossie's money, opened the sack and gave them six crisp, shiny bagels.

The children ate ravenously.

"Don't eat so fast!" The bagel woman wagged a finger at them. "You'll get indigestion."

"I can't help it," Becky spluttered with her mouth full. "They're so good."

They walked along together, chewing happily. Then Becky stopped suddenly and looked at her brother.

"Wait a minute," she frowned. "I've just remembered. Bubbe didn't have any change this morning, so where d'you get the money?"

Yossie's mouth was too full to speak.

"From Papa?"

He shook his head.

"Did you find it?"

Yossie swallowed. "No, I didn't," he protested.

"You're a sly one, Yossie Feldman. Stop stuffing your mouth will you, and tell me."

"You'll only get mad, so I'm not telling."

"Mad? Me? Don't be daft. I won't, I promise."

Yossie looked at Mirrie. "You heard what she said."

He finished eating and wiped his mouth on his sleeve. "Sol Haffner gave me the money," he said, looking nervously at his sister. "I didn't ask him for it, honest. He just gave it to me."

"Sol Haffner? I don't believe you. Sol Haffner?" She repeated. "That bully gave you two pennies? Is that the honest truth?"

"Yeah."

"If I'd known that before, I'd've spat them out! Don't you ever take money from him or any of that family again. D'you hear me?"

"Oh leave him alone, Becky. What're you getting mad at Yossie, for?" Mirrie asked. "He didn't do anything wrong. Look, it's getting late and I've got to get home and help Mama. Come on both of you and stop squabbling."

★ ★ ★

Becky was boiling with anger. How dare Sol Haffner try to bribe her brother! She was sure his mother had put him up to it. "Yossie's too young to understand what's going on, but I do," she muttered.

By the time she got to the bakers, it was packed with cholent customers. She could see Mirrie ahead of her waiting in line. Suddenly a voice called out behind her.

"Becky Feldman, is that you? Hey! You! Becky Feldman!" Becky looked round. A young girl waved to her.

"Can you hear me? I've got a message for your grandmother."

Becky blinked in surprise. It was Dora, the youngest of the Haffner girls. Before she could say anything, the girl shouted: "Mama, I mean Mrs Haffner, wants you all to come over for *Shabbos* dinner tomorrow. Don't forget to tell your grandmother and your father."

Becky blushed scarlet. Why did Dora have to shout about it at the top of her voice? She didn't know where to look. *The gossips are going to love this*, she thought bitterly. As soon as she handed the cholent over, she snatched the tag and rushed out of the shop. Mirrie was waiting for her.

"Oh, I could just kill that Dora Haffner," Becky raged, holding her hands up to her burning cheeks.

"Why, what's up? What d'you mean?" Mirrie asked.

"She said we've got to go and eat cholent with Mrs Haffner

tomorrow. Why did she have to tell everyone and show me up in front of all those people?"

"Oh, don't be so touchy, Becky," Mirrie told her. "Look out, here she comes." Dora stopped, looked down and shuffled her feet awkwardly.

"We're that busy at home, I didn't have time to *shlep* round to your place," she mumbled. "Then I saw you in the line. I…I…didn't mean any harm. My mother's expecting you all, see you tomorrow."

Becky glared at the girl. She couldn't trust herself to speak.

"Well, she sort of said she was sorry, didn't she?" Mirrie asked.

"I was so humiliated," Becky blurted out. "I could have died of shame."

"What's got into you, Becky? What are you getting so upset about?"

Becky didn't answer. They walked along in silence. Then suddenly, she stopped, pressed her back against a wall and folded her arms.

"You don't understand, Mirrie," Becky felt the tears at the back of her throat. "You just don't understand," she repeated. "I'm in terrible trouble and I don't know what to do."

"I'll help you if I can, you know I will," Mirrie said gently.

"Promise you won't tell a soul?"

"Course not. I'm your friend, aren't I?"

Mirrie's kind words seemed to unlock something deep inside her. All the worries that she had kept bottled up for so long came pouring out. She told Mirrie everything from the time when Bubbe suddenly announced that they should have a new mother, Abe Klein and Mrs Haffner, to the gossips in the public baths. When she had finished Becky felt that a heavy weight had been lifted from her shoulders.

"It's such a relief to talk to you, Mirrie. Now you know what I'm up against. Sol Haffner's trying to *shmooze* Yossie. I'm sure his mother's behind it. Why else would he give Yossie that money? Worst of all, we've got to go there tomorrow. You know why, don't you?"

"So you can all meet Mrs Haffner's family?"

"Yeah, she'll go on and on about her wonderful children. It makes me feel sick just thinking about it."

"What does your father say?"

"He won't talk to me about it, he's told me not to meddle in grown up things. That's why it's so hard to find out what's going on."

"Well, tomorrow he'll find out what he's in for. If he marries Mrs Haffner he'll suddenly find he has five more kids to care for!"

"I won't share my father with those Haffners, I won't," Becky said fiercely. She pretended to fiddle with the cholent tag in her pocket so Mirrie wouldn't see her wet cheeks.

"Hey, now just you wait a minute, Becky."

Becky wiped her eyes. "What?" she sniffed.

"Well, I thought you said Mrs Haffner is supposed to be a bad cook! Didn't you hear some gossip in the public baths yesterday?"

Becky's expression changed. "You're right, yes," she repeated slowly, "you're right. How stupid of me to have forgotten that! I must be going crazy." Her eyes grew wide and slowly her face lit up in a big smile.

"I can't wait to see Papa's face tomorrow when he eats Mrs Herring's rotten, dried up cholent. If anything's going to change his mind, that will. He loves his food. D'you know, Mirrie, I feel better already."

"Good! Now you can forget about tomorrow, and think

about the delicious dinner you'll have tonight instead."

"Tonight? What's so special about tonight?"

"Mama's a very good cook."

"Your mother? What are you talking about?"

"Didn't Bubbe tell you that Mama wants you to come and eat with us tonight?"

"Tonight? Me? Really? Bubbe didn't tell me, I expect she forgot."

"You were out when I asked her, but she said it would be alright. Will you come?"

"Oh yes, thanks. I'll wear the dress Hester gave me."

"That's settled then. Come on, it's cold standing here. Oh, that reminds me. You'll have to bring something to sit on, 'cos we haven't got enough chairs!"

They grinned at each other, linked arms and ran home.

★ ★ ★

Becky could only see her head and neck in the small, cracked kitchen mirror. She smoothed down her hair and patted the new collar in place. She pinched her cheeks to get some colour into them like she'd seen Hester doing. She smiled at her reflection. *I'm not being vain*, she thought, *but I think I look quite nice*. She tried to get a better view of herself as she passed the shiny samovar, but it made her look a funny shape.

"Good *Shabbos*, everyone. I'm going up to Mrs Lazarus's now." She tried not to sound too excited. Then she took a deep breath and announced: "Bubbe, Dora Haffner told me at the bakers today that her mother is expecting us all for dinner tomorrow." Then, without waiting to see how the invitation was received, she grabbed a stool, opened the door and closed it quietly behind her.

Becky stood outside number 139 clutching her wooden stool. She wiped her boots against the back of her stockings, balancing first on one leg and then the other. When they looked clean enough, she tapped on the door.

"Good *Shabbos*, Becky, how nice you look," Mrs Lazarus smiled. "Come in, come in." Becky, feeling a little nervous and shy, sat down next to Mirrie. Two young men were standing near the fire, talking and laughing. The taller one had flaming red hair and a beard to match.

"Dov and Alex are family friends," Mrs Lazarus explained. "They looked after us on the journey. We couldn't have managed without them, especially as the boat was full of rogues and thieves."

"D'you know what Mama did?" Mirrie burst in.

Becky shook her head.

"She sewed all her savings into the lining of her coat and wore it all the time. She even slept in it!" Mirrie giggled. "One of the ladies I got to know told me that she'd sewn her money inside her corset! I know you're funny about smells, Becky," she went on, "but you just can't imagine what a stench there was down below. We were packed in like sardines and everyone was seasick and…"

"Spare us the details, Mirrie dear," Mrs Lazarus interrupted quickly. "It's dinner time and I'm sure our *Shabbos* guests are hungry."

Before the meal was served, Dov read the blessings, poured the wine, sprinkled salt on the challah and handed it round.

"Have you ever seen Tower Bridge, Becky?" Alex asked, stabbing his fork into his food. Becky couldn't help noticing that his carrots were almost the same colour as his hair and his beard!

"No."

"Well we have," he said, his eyes shining with excitement. "I still can't believe it. The day we arrived in England there was such a thick fog we couldn't see a thing. We could hear fog horns all around us, but we'd no idea where we were. Suddenly the fog lifted and there we were, sailing up the River Thames surrounded by all kinds of boats – passenger ships like ours, freighters, sailing boats, and rowing boats. Then I saw this gigantic bridge stretching right across the river. What a sight! D'you know what happened next?"

Becky shook her head.

"As we got nearer, the bridge seemed to split down the middle and the two halves went up in the air like this." He dropped his knife and fork and raised his arms slowly above his head to show her how the bridge worked. "Then all the ships just sailed through. Magic! It was magic," he repeated.

"After that, we had a perfect view of the Tower of London!" Dov added. "What a wonderful sight that was."

"Well I remember quite a different sight." Mrs Lazarus sighed as if she was reliving the moment. "I hate to think what we must have looked like when we landed at the Tilbury Docks. Hundreds of us poor Russian Jews, hungry and dirty, all shuffling slowly down the gangway clutching our bags and bundles. Thank God my aunt was there to meet us."

"We're lucky too," Alex said. "We live in a free country, thank God, we've got jobs so we can save up to bring our families here. Which reminds me, Mrs Lazarus, have you heard from Hershel?"

"Yes I have," Mrs Lazarus smiled and flushed with pleasure. "I got a letter from him three days ago. I told you all about my good friend Hershel who lives in America, didn't I Becky? Well now he's written to tell me that he's coming to England. I'm so excited, I can't think of anything else these days!"

"When is he coming?" Alex asked.

"Hershel's plans keep changing, so it's hard to know exactly. America is so far away; I must learn to be patient and not to get too excited. It'll be so good to see him after all these years." Her face lit up at the prospect.

"Now, what are we waiting for?" Alex asked, banging his fist down on the table and making Becky jump. "It's time for some *Shabbos* songs."

★ ★ ★

Flat 74 Rothschild Buildings,
Brick Lane,
Whitechapel,
London.

Friday 20th November 1908

Dear Mama,

Oy vey! Real trouble! Our new washerwoman was drunk! She stank of gin; she nearly fell over when she came in. She just dumped the bundle of clean washing on the floor, took her money and staggered out. After she'd gone we realised that she'd got everything mixed up. My things were alright but Papa had to wear someone else's shirt which was too small for him. He looked so funny, I had to bite my tongue to stop myself laughing! Yossie got the giggles because he got a shirt with sleeves so long he looked like a monkey! We'll have to wait until after Shabbos to sort it out.

I had a lovely dinner with Mirrie, her mother and their friends. Mrs Lazarus has a good friend in America called Hershel who is going to come and see her. From the way she was talking about him, I think she's expecting to marry him.

Now – for the Secrets Of My Heart. We're going to the Haffners after shul tomorrow. I hope and pray that Mrs H's cholent will taste so awful that it will really put Papa off.

I miss you very much. God bless.

Yours faithfully,

Rebecca Feldman.

Chapter 9

"You look all washed out, Becky. What's up?" Meg asked, sweeping up the ashes in the hearth.

"Bubbe kept me awake half the night, moaning in her sleep," Becky yawned, rubbing her eyes.

"I keeps tellin' you. That bedroom's too cold for 'er, damp too, I shouldn't wonder. Right then, let's get 'er in 'ere," Meg said, pointing to the alcove.

"What?"

"If she's got arthritis, she 'as to be kept warm. I knows all about it, 'cos me grandad was bad with it. I'll warm the beddin'."

She pulled back the alcove curtain, stripped the blankets from the bed and hung them over the fire-guard in front of the fire. Becky looked at the empty bed. It hadn't been used since her mama was ill. She turned away quickly and started rummaging in the dresser.

"We've got a spare sheet somewhere," she muttered, pulling one out of the bottom drawer. "Will this do?"

"Yeah. 'Ave you got a hot water bottle?"

Becky fetched the stone bottle from the kitchen, filled it with hot water from the samovar and wrapped it in a cloth.

"Give it me," Meg said putting it under the blankets. "She'll be warm and cosy in 'ere. Come on, let's go and get 'er."

Slowly and carefully, they led Bubbe to the alcove bed.

"There now," Meg said, plumping up the pillows. "You'll be much better off in 'ere, Mrs Feldman. Cup of tea?"

Bubbe nodded. She pulled her shawl round her shoulders.

"Aaah," she sighed. "That's good, it was so cold in there. Becky, thank Meg and see what you can find to give her."

"D'you want some breakfast, Bubbe?" Becky asked when Meg had gone.

"I'm not hungry, just very tired. You're such good girls, both of you, looking after me so well," she tried to smile.

Breakfast was eaten quietly so as not to disturb her. Only the rustling of Papa's newspaper and the fire crackling in the grate broke the silence. Papa leaned across the table.

"Becky, you'd better stay home with Bubbe," he whispered. "Are you ready, Yossie? Come, we're late."

The minute the door closed, she remembered – Mrs. Haffner's Invitation!!

"Too late, too late!" she muttered. *Stupid, stupid girl*! she told herself. *I forgot to remind Papa. I can't leave Bubbe but I don't want to miss it all. I've just got to see Papa's face when he eats Mrs Haffner's dried up cholent.* She sat gazing into the glowing embers of the fire, not knowing what to do.

There was a gentle tap on the door. Becky looked up and watched it opening slowly. A hand appeared holding a pair of boots, followed by a grinning face.

"'Ow's your grandmother?" Meg asked.

"Shhh! Meg! What are you doing here? I thought you'd gone home ages ago. Come in quick and shut the door, you're letting the cold in."

Meg padded softly across the room and sat down next to Becky.

"I've just finished cleaning up for Mrs Lazarus," she said quietly. "Look what she gave me," she said, holding up the boots. "They used to belong to Mr Kaminsky. He died a while back. They're too big for me, so I stuffed them with newspaper and they're fine now. D'you know what Mrs Lazarus told me?"

"Was it about Hershel?"

"Oh yeah, she's told me a lot about her American friend. It's not that though. She's going to start making dinners for them young men and a few others too when word gets round. She'll charge them, y'know, about four pence each, I think she said. That way she'll be able to save up and rent somewhere bigger and start a little catering business. She wants me to come in and 'elp 'er," Meg said proudly. "I'll be earning a bit extra so me Mam'll be pleased."

"I don't suppose they're still at home?" Becky asked anxiously.

"You've missed 'em. They went out half an hour since."

Becky was getting desperate.

"Have you got to go home now?" she asked.

Meg shrugged. "Dunno, why?"

"We've been invited to eat cholent with some people after *shul* and Bubbe's not well enough to go."

"Damn right she isn't! She'll catch 'er death of cold if she goes out in this weather. I'll stay with 'er, don't worry, I won't be missed at 'ome."

"Thanks Meg, that'll be such a help. Look, here's the cholent tag. Can you go down to the bakers for it while I get a few things ready? You and Bubbe can have an early dinner."

"I've never heard of cholent," Meg looked puzzled," I didn't know the baker sold it."

"He doesn't. Every Friday Bubbe prepares the cholent, a sort of beef stew, and I take it to the baker who puts it in his big oven to cook slowly overnight. We can't cook it here because we can't keep the fire going on *Shabbos*."

"Like I keep on saying, Becky, you're a grand little teacher! I shan't be long."

★ ★ ★

By the time Meg returned, Bubbe was awake. She looked pale and drawn with pain. Meg was right, she was too ill to go out.

"Becky dear," she winced. "Tell Mrs Haffner that I've got one of my bad days. She's a good woman, she'll understand. You'll meet all the children and enjoy yourselves there."

"I'm sure I will," Becky coughed. "I'd better be going now. Meg'll look after the fire and keep the cholent hot until you're ready to eat it."

"Wrap up warm Becky, it's terrible out there," Meg warned her. "Don't worry about your grandmother, I'll look after her. I'm looking forward to the cholent!"

It'll be much, much nicer than the one I'm going to eat, Becky thought.

"Thanks for everything, Meg."

It was bitterly cold and damp and a thick fog had wrapped itself tightly around the buildings like a dark grey blanket. Becky could hardly see her hand when she held it up in front of her. It was eerie and strangely quiet. Everyday sounds were muffled. People appeared suddenly like ghostly shapes, then vanished just as quickly. She walked slowly, stopping every now and then to peer ahead, looking for familiar landmarks. Suddenly, without warning, she felt a horse's hot breath on the back of her head. She must have strayed on to the road. Quick as a flash, she leapt out of its way. She stood trembling with fear, her heart pounding. She groped her way to a wall and leant against it until she felt calmer.

She set off again, trailing her fingers along the railings of the tenement buildings to guide her. Then she felt a knot of panic in the pit of her stomach. *Papa thinks I'm at home with Bubbe and he doesn't know I'm coming. Suppose I miss him? Suppose I get lost trying to find the Haffner's place?* She stopped again and took a deep breath. "Pull yourself together right now, Becky Feldman," she told herself sternly. "You know the way perfectly well – why you could find it blindfolded!" Which was just what it felt like.

Soon after, she made out the familiar outline of the synagogue building against the dark sky. *I couldn't have timed it better*, she thought, as the great doors swung open at the end of the service. There were no big crowds today and even the gossips were in a hurry to get home, as it was too cold to hang about. Only a brief "Good *Shabbos*," to one another before family groups were quickly swallowed up in the fog.

At last Becky saw Papa and Yossie. She was just explaining to Papa about Meg staying with Bubbe when Abe Klein appeared, as if from nowhere.

"Good *Shabbos*. What do you think of this pea-souper, eh Yossie?"

"What's a pea-souper?"

"Does your Bubbe make you pea soup?"

"Sometimes."

"Is it very thick?"

"Yeah."

"Well, as you can see, so is this fog," Abe Klein laughed. "Follow me. I know the way."

It was easier said than done. One moment Becky could see the back of him, the next he had disappeared. Nagging thoughts crossed her mind as they struggled to keep up with him. She should have guessed that Abe Klein knew about Mrs Herring's invitation. Perhaps he'd arranged it. After all, wasn't that part of his job?

"I can't breathe properly in this pea-soup fog, or whatever it's called," Yossie whimpered, coughing and choking. "Are we nearly there, Becky? I'm starving."

"It's not far now, I'm sure it's just round the next corner." She tucked his arm through hers and gave his hand a big squeeze. *You'll be hungry enough to eat anything*, she smiled to herself.

★ ★ ★

Mrs Haffner was waiting for them at the side entrance – a great relief to Becky, who dreaded having to go through the shop.

"Good *Shabbos,* good *Shabbos.* What a terrible day!" she fussed." Come in and get warm."

A fine lace cloth covered the large dining room table. Becky was impressed with the way the candlesticks shone like burnished gold. Much better than her efforts, she had to admit. Large framed photographs of fierce-looking Haffner relatives decorated the walls. Whenever she looked up they seemed to be glaring down at her, their eyes following her around the room. The Haffner children were scrubbed, sullen and silent. Becky could tell they'd been warned, or bribed, to be on their best behaviour. Dora gave her a shy smile. Sol scowled as he stood back to allow the guests to get near the fire. *They must be hating us as much as I'm hating them*, she thought to herself.

Mrs Haffner opened a cupboard in the large dresser and took out some glasses and a bottle of whisky.

"Y'know, my late husband, God rest his soul, used to say that there's nothing quite like a little drop of whisky to keep out the cold," she smiled, pouring out a drink for the two men.

"Thank you, Mrs Haffner." Abe Klein took his glass and emptied it in one swallow. "Aah, good stuff! Just what the doctor ordered!" He laughed loudly at his own joke.

Becky watched her father sipping his drink in silence. *He doesn't look as if he's enjoying himself*, she thought, more like it was something he'd rather get over and done with.

"God bless you and your wonderful children, Mrs Haffner. They are a real credit to you," Abe Klein *shmoozed*. "Now I…"

"Thank you, Mr Klein," she interrupted, "it's good of you to say so. I'm very proud of Sol and Mat, they're such good boys. I don't know what I'd do without my lovely girls, Sophie, Bessy and Dora. They're always ready to help me out in the shop when I'm busy," she babbled on. Becky's heart sank. She dreaded what was sure to come next.

"And what d'you think of Jacob's marvellous children, eh?" Abe Klein asked. He put a heavy hand on Yossie's shoulder, making him squirm. "Yossie's going to be a rabbi when he grows up, aren't you my boy?"

Becky managed a warning look at Yossie. What was that awful man going to say next, she wondered, cringing inside.

"Everyone in the Rothschild Buildings knows what a great help Becky is to her Bubbe," Abe Klein went on. "And what a clever girl! Top of the class in English and trying for a scholarship next year. She…"

To Becky's great relief, Abe Klein was stopped from making any more embarrassing remarks when Mrs Haffner announced: "Come and sit down everyone, the dinner's ready. You must all be very hungry."

★ ★ ★

Flat 74 Rothschild Buildings,
Brick Lane,
Whitechapel,
London.

Saturday 21ˢᵗ November 1908

Dear Mama,

The Secrets Of My Heart! Mrs Haffner's cholent was absolutely delicious!! I couldn't believe it at first. The meat was tender with lots of gravy and Papa's favourite dumplings. Everything was just as if you had made it yourself. I had to sit there and watch Papa enjoy every mouthful, he even smiled at Mrs Haffner when she gave him a second helping. I couldn't eat mine, it stuck in my throat.

I sobbed my heart out when I got home. I'll never call Mrs Herring 'mama.' I can't imagine ever wanting to kiss and hug her. She's the kind of woman who'll be saying, "No buts, Becky" all the time. I'm in despair.

All my love Mama. God bless.

Yours faithfully,

Rebecca Feldman.

Chapter 10

NO, NO! Becky silently framed these words as she stood shivering at her door, listening to Papa talking to Bubbe

"Rabbi Meyer wants to see me this afternoon," he said. "I'm not sure what time I'll be home."

Rabbi Meyer! That could only mean one thing. Papa had stopped thinking it over. He was going to get married! "Please God, don't let this happen," she whispered.

She walked in and stood warming her hands by the fire. She looked closely at her father. He doesn't look any different. Shouldn't he look happy? It was all very strange.

"Are you feeling better, Bubbe?" she asked, cutting herself a slice of bread.

"Don't remind me about yesterday. *Oy vey!* Such pain! Today, thanks be to God, I feel much better. Yossie, my child, eat up, eat up," she fussed, as he came in and sat down at the table. "Your father's got to go out. He'll take you to cheder."

"I...I..." Yossie hesitated. He looked at Papa, then at Bubbe and then at Becky. He tried again. "I...I...don't..." then stopped. Becky could see that he was close to tears. He looked so desperate. *Poor kid*, she thought, *it's not fair, making him go there.* She took a deep breath.

"Papa, I think you should talk to Rebbe Finegold. He shouts at the boys and hits them and Yossie gets upset. Can't he go somewhere else to learn Hebrew?"

Papa ignored her. He folded his newspaper without a word and put on his coat. *I don't care if he's angry with me,* Becky said to herself, *I promised Yossie I'd stick up for him.*

"Have you finished eating?" Papa asked.

Yossie nodded.

"Come on then." He opened the front door and turned around to glare at her.

"I won't tell you again, Becky. Don't meddle in matters which don't concern you, or Yossie or anyone else."

"But...!"

"No buts, Becky," he snapped.

Yossie glanced back at her as he hurried after his father. *Thanks for trying*, his look seemed to say.

"Rebbe Finegold's a very cruel man, Bubbe," Becky protested.

"Now, don't take on so, Becky. Yossie'll be alright. Rebbe Finegold's a good teacher. He's very strict with the boys, that's all. He needs to be, teaching that mob!" She poured herself another cup of tea.

"What a shame I couldn't come with you yesterday," Bubbe chatted, quickly changing the subject. "Such a lovely family, God bless them. Mrs Haffner told me she was going to use her best *Shabbos* cloth – the lace one. It was all hand stitched by her mother and her aunts." She sipped her tea noisily. "Your mother had a lovely one too, but it was pawned a long time ago," she sighed.

"Did Papa say he enjoyed himself?" Becky asked, trying to sound offhand.

"Now what kind of a question is that, eh? Course he did. After all, what's not to enjoy! That reminds me, Becky, there's plenty of cholent left over from yesterday. I'll heat it up again for dinner."

Oh please, don't mention cholent! Becky felt like screaming. She didn't want to see any more of it as long as she lived! Just then there was a knock at the door. It was Mirrie.

"How are you, Mrs Feldman?" Mirrie asked.

"Mustn't complain, mustn't complain. I'm much better today, thank God."

"Can Becky come with me to the market? The fog's lifted, so we'll be able to see what we're buying!"

"Get my purse, Becky. Go along with Mirrie and get me a few things. Leave the dishes," she said, as Becky started to clear up. "It'll give me something to do. I can't be sitting around doing nothing all day."

★ ★ ★

"I'm so glad you came, Mirrie," Becky sighed as they walked arm in arm to the market, "because I'm in the depths of despair."

"What d'you mean, 'in the depths of despair'? What's up? I thought you'd be feeling very pleased with yourself today. Now look at you, all pale and washed out. What happened?"

"I can't bear to talk about it."

"For heaven's sake, Becky, tell me!"

"Mrs Herring Haffner's cholent was delicious! It was just as good as my mother's used to be!" Becky blurted out.

"No! Honestly?"

Becky nodded.

"Poor Becky, I'm very sorry," Mirrie said, trying to comfort her friend. "The gossips in the public baths must have got it wrong."

"I was stupid enough to believe them. You can't imagine how terrible it was for me having to sit there listening to everyone going on about Mrs H being a wonderful cook. It made me want to throw up. Abe Klein said – "

"Abe Klein?" Mirrie interrupted. "What was he doing there?"

"He must have arranged it all, 'cos Papa wouldn't have gone on his own."

"Look, Becky, I don't think you should…"

"Papa's going to marry her," Becky said quietly.

"What, already? So soon?"

"Yes, I think so. He's going to speak to Rabbi Meyer about it today."

"How d'you know that?"

"I heard him telling Bubbe."

"What did he say?"

"Only that he was going to see the rabbi."

"Well it may not be about getting married. Rabbis look after all sorts of other things, y'know."

Becky sniffed and wiped her eyes on the corner of her apron.

"I still think Papa's mad. Yossie'll be alright, it'll be different for him. She'll give him lots of food and spoil him."

"What about your grandmother?"

Becky shrugged. "I don't know if Mrs Haffner'll be able to look after her. Anyway, I've made up my mind," she said defiantly, "I'm not going to live with them. I'd run away like a shot, if I'd got somewhere to go."

The girls stopped and looked at each other as if one single thought had struck them at the same time.

"Come and live with us!" Mirrie beamed. "Mama likes you. She's always talking about you."

"Is she? Really?" Becky said shyly. "She made me feel so much at home on Friday. But have you got room for me?"

"Course we have. Mrs K has one room and Mum and I share a bed in the other. You can have the alcove bed and…" Mirrie stopped as if she'd just remembered something. "My mother's friend Hershel's coming all the way from America to see us, though I don't know when exactly."

"I've heard so much about him from your mother. What's he like?"

"I don't remember because I was too little. He must be fond of Mama because he's always kept in touch with her. D'you want to come to us, then?"

"Oh, Mirrie, you know I would."

Mirrie squeezed Becky's arm excitedly. "Good, I'll ask Mama and see what she says. We'll be able to do our homework and have fun together. But what you need now," she said, opening her purse, "is a little treat. D'you want a slice of coconut?"

"Ooh yes!"

"Come on then, I'll buy some. Cheer up, I hate seeing you all upset."

They wandered round eating, chatting and shopping. They had almost finished when Mirrie stopped and nudged Becky.

"Look, Becky, look over there!"

"Who? Where?"

"There, there, just in front of the book stall. Isn't that your father talking to someone?"

Becky went white as a sheet.

"That's Abe Klein," she hissed. "Oh, God, Papa doesn't

waste any time does he? He must be telling him about meeting the rabbi. Quick, Mirrie, let's go. I don't want them to see us."

They mingled with the crowds of shoppers along the rows of market stalls. They were just about to turn the corner when they bumped straight into Sol Haffner. Quick as a flash, he grabbed Becky by the hair.

"Ouch, you're hurting me!" she shouted. "Get off me! Leave me alone!" She wriggled and squirmed and kicked, but Sol held her fast.

Mirrie tried to grab his arm. "Let go of her, you great bully, let her go," she screamed.

"Shurrup, you!" Sol growled. He shoved her roughly out of the way without losing his grip on Becky.

"So this is the precious scholarship girl, is it?" he sneered, putting his face close to hers. "My sisters don't go in for fancy learning. They 'ave to work at home and in the shop, got that? D'you want to know what happens to girls who get too big for their boots?" he asked, giving Becky's hair another sharp pull. "Do you?" he shouted. "No? Well I'll show you…"

★ ★ ★

Flat 74 Rothschild Buildings,
Brick Lane,
Whitechapel,
London.

Sunday 22nd November 1908

Dear Mama,

The Secrets Of My Heart (although this time it isn't very secret!)

81

Sol Haffner knocked me flying in the market today. I fell backwards, crashing into a market stall with fruit and vegetables pouring down on me. I cut my eye which swelled up until I couldn't see out of it. My nose was bleeding, my knees were grazed and I hurt my back. I just lay there shivering and shaking all over. Mirrie screamed for help and then suddenly there were lots of people round us. One of the neighbours from our building took us home. Bubbe was very upset and sent Mirrie to buy a piece of beef steak to put on my eye to get the swelling down. Yossie said it was a waste of good meat! (Well, he would wouldn't he?) I wish Papa had been there. He keeps asking me how I'm feeling, but that's all. He's gone quieter than ever.

I'm still covered in bruises and my bad eye is like the colours of the rainbow: black, blue, red, green and a bit of yellow. I can't bear to look in the mirror. Everyone at school knows about it. Sol Haffner denied everything, he said I'd tripped and fallen. He's a liar and a bully. My friends are very kind, they keep giving me special treats – toffee apples and cinnamon buns, which I share with Yossie and Mirrie. Miss Bennet told me not to do any homework until my eye's better. Mrs Lazarus washed the mud off my dress and mended my torn petticoat and stockings.

My mind is quite made up. I'm never going to live with the Haffners, not after what happened. Mirrie is going to ask her mother and Mrs K if I can live with them. Please ask God to help me with my plan, because I don't know what else I can do.

God Bless.

Yours faithfully,

Rebecca Feldman.

Chapter 11

"You'd better get upstairs quick, Becky. Mirrie wants you," Meg announced the moment she opened the door.

"Why?"

"She's got summat to tell you."

Becky frowned and shook her head. "I can't leave Bubbe, she's really bad today. Papa told me to stay home with her."

"I'll keep an eye on 'er while I'm clearing up the breakfast pots." She peeped behind the alcove curtain. "She's fast asleep. I'll make 'er a cup of tea when she wakes up. Go on 'urry up. I'll stay on until you bring the cholent back from the bakers."

"Thanks Meg." She dashed up the steps two at a time and met Mrs Lazarus on her way down.

"How are you dear?" She cupped Becky's face in her hands and looked closely at her black eye.

"Hmmm!" she murmured, tilting Becky's head first this

way and then that. "It's much better. Does it still hurt?" she asked, letting her go.

"Not so much now."

"Good. By this time next week, your eye will be quite better and you'll have forgotten all about it."

Becky shook her head. "No I won't, Mrs Lazarus. I'll never forget what happened, or who did it," she answered quickly.

"Becky, I..." she hesitated. She looked as if she was going to say something important, then changed her mind. She shivered.

"You're going to see Mirrie, yes? Well hurry up before you catch cold. I must go now, I'm late. Good *Shabbos*."

Mirrie was waiting for her. Her eyes were red and she looked upset.

"What's up with you?" Becky asked. "If my Auntie Essie was here she'd say you look as if you'd got out of bed on the wrong side! What's happened? Have you had a row with your mother? She was a bit odd when I saw her just now."

Mirrie shook her head. "No, nothing like that. It's just that...well, d'you remember when you told me you were going to run away?"

"Yes, why?"

"I asked Mama if you could come and live with us and she said..." Mirrie stopped and put her hand on her throat as if she had trouble getting the words out.

"She doesn't want me, does she? Is that what you're trying to tell me?"

"It wasn't like that, Becky. Honestly, you've got to believe me," Mirrie pleaded. "Mama likes you very much, you know that. She was so upset when she saw your black eye and everything. It's...it's...well, the thing is, she said your father would never give his permission to let you live with a family he doesn't know very well. He knows Mrs K, but he's never even met my mother."

"That's true. You're right. He's never even met your mother," Becky repeated, as if she was talking to herself.

The two girls sat staring at the flickering flames. The clock ticking away on the dresser was the only sound in the room. Becky's mind was racing; she was working on a daring new plan.

She sat up suddenly and looked at Mirrie.

"Well, it looks as if I'll have to start meddling again, doesn't it?"

Mirrie's eyes were shining with excitement.

"I know what you're thinking, Becky."

"Do you?"

"Yes, I do, honest I do!"

"And d'you think it's a good idea?"

"Course I do!" she burst out laughing.

"Right then. We've got to be quick. You know what Miss Bennet would say, 'Now listen carefully girls and pay attention!' they chanted together.

★ ★ ★

Not long afterwards the girls stood breathless outside Becky's door, two pots of cholent on the floor between them.

"Are you quite sure you know what you've got to do?" Becky asked, trying to get her breath back.

"For goodness sake," Mirrie gasped. "How many more times have I got to tell you! I know my instructions inside out, back to front, off by heart."

Becky bit her nails. "Suppose your mother doesn't get

back in time?" she said, beginning to feel uneasy.

"I keep telling you, she's only gone to the next building to help the family with the new baby. She told me she's just going to take them some food and see they're alright and come straight back home."

"Well don't wait for her," Becky ordered. "Start eating Bubbe's cholent as soon as you get in. Just say you were starving. Tell her we were talking so much we didn't notice the cholents got mixed up. She won't mind. She'll understand. You've just got to make sure that your mother returns Bubbe's empty pot, not you. Whatever happens don't let her send you down instead."

"I know, I know."

They looked at the pots, then at each other and started to giggle.

"I'm going to wet myself if I go on like this!" Becky spluttered. "Oh, God, I hope it'll all work out. Papa'll go mad when he finds out."

Just then Meg opened the door.

"I thought I heard you two carryin' on out 'ere. Bubbe's awake but she doesn't want a cup of tea. I'd best be off now. See you next week. Good *Shabbos*."

Mirrie bent down and gripped the cloth tied round Bubbe's pot. She turned to go upstairs.

"Don't worry, Becky, it'll be fine. See you later. Good luck!"

"Thanks, I'll need it."

Please God, please make it work, she prayed quietly. She carried Mrs Lazarus's cholent inside and put it carefully on the table. The carrying cloth had yellowed in the heat of the baker's oven, just like their own. Bubbe wouldn't know the difference until she ate it. *I'll have to think of something to say then*, she thought. She heard groaning from behind the alcove curtain and drew it aside.

"Does your knee hurt?" she asked.

Bubbe sucked in her breath sharply.

"It'll pass, it'll pass," she moaned.

"D'you want something to eat, or a hot drink?"

"Nothing, dear, not now. Just leave me. It'll pass."

Becky tidied her bedclothes and closed the curtains. She felt sorry for Bubbe, but relieved she wasn't hungry. Moments later she heard footsteps.

As soon as Papa and Yossie walked in she put her finger to her lips to warn them. "Shhh!" she whispered, "Bubbe's resting."

She waited for Papa to wash his hands, recite the blessings, and hand round the challah. Then with trembling hands she lifted the lid off Mrs Lazarus's piping hot cholent. They breathed in the wonderful aroma of the savoury stew.

"Mmmm! What a lovely smell," Yossie drooled. "Hurry up, Becky, my stomach's rumbling."

Becky heaped the stew on to their plates, making sure that Papa had a generous portion of dumplings.

The cholent was cooked to perfection. She could tell from the way they ate that Papa and Yossie thought so too.

"I can't understand it," Papa said quietly, slicing a dumpling in half. "I just can't understand," he repeated, "how your grandmother managed to make such a wonderful cholent, when she's not been well. She's even made my favourite dumplings. We haven't had them for ages."

Becky blushed. *Oy vey! I'm sure I'll be in big trouble when he finds out that I've been meddling again*, she thought.

"More please," Yossie held out his plate. Becky dished out a second helping for him and Papa, and put some aside in a small pot for Bubbe. When the last of the gravy had been mopped up with bread and their plates scraped clean, Papa said grace and Becky cleared the table. She looked at the clock and then at her father. *Don't go to sleep now, please stay awake*, she prayed.

Becky's eyes kept going back to the clock as if they were drawn there by a magnet. The time seemed to stand still. She strained to listen out for footsteps on the stairs. A knock on the door made her jump.

"Who can that be?" Papa asked, half rising from his chair. "We're not expecting anyone."

"I'll go, Papa, I'll go. I expect it's someone who wants you to read a letter, or translate something," Becky lied, trying to sound casual. She longed to dash across the room, but forced herself to walk.

Mrs Lazarus stood smiling in the doorway. She held Bubbe's empty cholent pot in one hand and a plate of biscuits in the other. Mirrie stood behind her, as if she was hiding.

"Oh, Mrs Lazarus, Good *Shabbos*, come in," Becky said, pretending to be surprised.

"Papa, this is Mrs Lazarus," Becky said nervously, "Mrs K's niece and my friend Mirrie's mother." Papa stood up. He looked embarrassed.

"Good *Shabbos*," he mumbled.

"Good *Shabbos*. I'm very sorry to disturb you, Mr Feldman," Mrs Lazarus said, putting the biscuits and the pot on the table, "but I came to explain that there's been some mistake. My cholent…" Before she could finish, there was a sharp cry of pain from the alcove. Becky quickly parted the curtains.

"Bubbe, what's the matter?"

"*Oy vey! Oy vey!*" Bubbe gasped. "Such stabbing pains!" she groaned, rubbing her knees.

"Let me help your grandmother, Becky. Have you got some wintergreen, Mrs Feldman?" Mrs Lazarus asked.

Bubbe shook her head.

"It's the best thing for arthritis, it helps to get the inflammation down. I've got a tin upstairs. I'll rub some on for you. D'you mind if I send Mirrie for it?" she asked Papa.

"That's kind of you," he murmured. "Thank you."

"Mirrie, bring me the strips of red flannel cloth. They're in the second drawer of the dresser. The wintergreen's on the top somewhere."

"What's wintergreen?" Mirrie asked.

"It's an ointment in a small, brown tin. Now where did I put it?" She thought for a moment. "Oh yes, I remember now. It's in the blue box on the right hand side of the dresser. You'll see it, Mirrie, it's just below my picture of Pochep. D'you know where I mean?"

Mirrie nodded.

"Be quick, then."

Mrs Lazarus wasted no time. She gently removed the stone hot water bottle from Bubbe's bed and unwrapped the cloth.

"This could do with some more hot water," she announced.

"I'll fill it," Papa said quickly, glad to be doing something useful.

Soon after, Mirrie returned with the ointment and the strips of red flannel cloth. Mrs Lazarus gently massaged Bubbe's knees with wintergreen and used the strips for bandages.

"There now, Mrs Feldman. I'm sure that'll ease the pain," she said. "I'll leave the tin here for you."

"That's very good of you, my dear," Bubbe managed a smile. "It feels easier already."

"Thank you, Mrs Lazarus, come and warm yourself," Papa said, moving a chair near the fire. "Becky, will you make some more tea?"

"Yes Papa," Becky replied. Mirrie rushed to help, happy to be kept busy. They handed round tea and biscuits, not daring to look at each other or show their feelings. Becky glanced quickly at Yossie who was grinning from ear to ear. Had he guessed she'd switched the cholents? From now on, her little brother must be watched very closely!

"Excuse me, Mrs Lazarus, but did you mention Pochep just now?" Papa asked shyly.

"Yes, I did. That's where Mirrie and I come from. My friend gave me a lovely drawing of Pochep before we left. Do you know it?"

"I knew a bookseller from Pochep, a real scholar. He often came to our little town."

"Then you must mean my father, Mendel Marshak!" Mrs Lazarus smiled proudly.

"You're…you're Mendel's daughter?" Papa blurted out in surprise. "Really?"

Mrs Lazarus nodded and smiled.

"I knew Mendel very well. If I didn't have enough money to buy the books I wanted, Mendel always let me pay for them whenever I could."

Becky looked at her father in amazement. She couldn't remember the last time he was so talkative.

"By the way, Mr Feldman," Mrs Lazarus said, pointing to Bubbe's pot on the table. "I really must explain about the mix up of the cholents."

The girls looked at each other. What if Yossie blurted out that Mrs Lazarus's cholent was better than Bubbe's? They couldn't take the risk, they had to act quickly. Mirrie opened the door. Becky grabbed Yossie, put her hand gently over his mouth and led him outside. They closed the door quietly behind them.

★ ★ ★

Flat 74 Rothschild Buildings,
Brick Lane,
Whitechapel,
London.

Saturday 28th November 1908

Dear Mama,

The Secrets Of My Heart! You would have been proud of me today, because this is the first time one of my meddling plans has worked out. When Papa marries Mrs Herring Haffner I'll go and live with Mrs K, Mirrie and Mrs Lazarus. She is very keen on education just like you were, so I'll be able to go on working for a scholarship. Papa has met her now so I don't think he'll mind so much. He hasn't said anything about his meeting with Rabbi Meyer. I just wish I knew what was going on. The bullies here have been taunting me shouting, "Good Shabbos, Rebecca Haffner!" I try my best to ignore them but, deep down, I get upset. I miss you very much.

All my love, God bless.

Yours faithfully,

Rebecca Feldman.

Chapter 12

"Pooh! This wintergreen stuff stinks of a hospital!" Becky wrinkled her nose and held the tin out as far away from herself as she could stretch.

"Smell or no smell, it's eased the pain in my legs," Bubbe told her. "Mrs Lazarus said she'd come down later on and rub some more on for me. What a godsend she was to me yesterday!" Bubbe nodded and smiled. "D'you know, Becky, she told me she's started a little catering business up there, making hot dinners for some friends of hers and a few others. I'm sure those men will appreciate a hot meal, don't you?"

Becky nodded. "Meg told me all about it. She goes up there to help Mrs Lazarus. Where's Papa?"

"He's gone to a meeting, then he said he's going upstairs to meet Mrs Lazarus's friends – Dov and Alex I think she said they were called. He might stop and have a bite to eat with them. They haven't been here very long, so they may have news of our relatives in Russia. They say no news is good news," Bubbe sighed, "but I'm not so sure about that and…"

A knock on the door stopped her mid-sentence.

"Hello! It's only me!" Auntie Essie popped her head round the door.

"I heard you hadn't been well, Bubbe, so I called to see how you're keeping. Just look who I've got with me, Becky!"

Becky, expecting Hester, was surprised to see Dora Haffner standing by the front door, shuffling her feet. She looked uncomfortable. *What's got into Auntie Essie, bringing her here?* she asked herself. She nodded at Dora, who managed a weak smile.

"Dora is Mrs Haffner's youngest girl, Bubbe." Auntie Essie explained. She turned to Becky. "I just happened to see her on my way here. She's going to the market to do a few errands for her auntie, so I thought you two girls could go together. That'll be nice for you, won't it?"

Becky didn't answer; she couldn't think of anything worse.

"Here you are," Auntie Essie rummaged in her purse, "buy a little treat for yourself and Yossie. I'll stay with Bubbe and heat up some chicken soup I've brought for her."

"I've got a lot of homework to finish before tomorrow," Becky grumbled, desperate to wriggle out of her aunt's plans. "I've…I've got a sore throat," she added lamely.

"It won't take long, Becky dear. You can have a hot drink and do your homework when you get back. Now go along with Dora. I'm sure you'll enjoy having a chat."

I certainly won't, Becky felt like shouting. In spite of her excuses, she would be forced to listen to Dora's chatter whether she liked it or not.

Dora wasted no time. "When your father and my mother

get…" she began, as soon as they were out of the building. She stopped, then began again. "I mean to say, when you all come to live with us, Sophie says we're going to be four in our bed. If you don't like that then you'll have to sleep on the floor."

"I'll let you know," Becky muttered, shuddering at the thought. Deep down she couldn't help comparing her choices! She was sure that when the time came to leave home, she'd get a comfortable bed and a warm welcome from Mrs K, Mrs Lazarus and Mirrie.

"My Auntie Zelda spoils me. I'm her favourite, y'know," Dora prattled on. "Look what she gave me for doing a few jobs," she boasted, taking a handful of coins out of her apron pocket. "She wants me to stay for dinner. She's a very good cook, y'know. Much better than my mother, but don't tell her I said so," she giggled. "Auntie Zelda used to cook for us when my father died. She doesn't so much now, only on special occasions."

"Special occasions?" Becky repeated, suddenly becoming very interested.

"Well y'know, if we've got important guests on *Shabbos*. She cooked for us once when Mama invited Abe Klein and this horrible man for dinner. It was a while back now, but I'll never forget that when he said grace after the meal he made it last for over half an hour!"

Becky could feel her heart racing with excitement. "And… and…when we came to dinner?" she asked, forcing herself to make her voice sound casual. "Was that a special occasion?"

"Course it was," Dora grinned. "Mama's always very busy in the shop these days, so she asked Auntie Zelda to make the cholent for her. She wanted to show off a bit, y'know. Well, there's no harm in that, is there?" she asked. She stopped suddenly and put her hand over mouth. "Oh me and my big mouth!" she gasped. "I forgot, I'm not supposed to say anything about that. You won't tell, will you Becky?" she pleaded.

Becky didn't answer. Dora's news came like a flash of lightning. *It's true, it's true*, she felt like shouting it out. Mrs Haffner didn't make that cholent! Dora had let the cat out of the bag, and she would never know how grateful Becky was. She had to tell Papa before it was too late. This news just had to make him change his mind.

"I…I've got to go home," Becky stammered.

Dora looked surprised. "I thought you were going to buy something for your brother?"

"I'll give him the money instead. He can buy his own treat. I've really got to get home, I've got a headache."

"You won't tell anyone what I said, will you?" Dora asked again.

What can I say? She asked herself. She didn't like telling lies, even though she'd been guilty of it recently. She had to find a good way round it.

"Don't worry about it. D'you know what my mother used to say?"

Dora shook her head.

"It's water under the bridge, now."

"What d'you mean?"

"It's best forgotten."

★ ★ ★

Bubbe stirred two teaspoonsful of honey into a cup of hot water.

"Here, Becky, sip this slowly, it'll soothe your sore throat."

"Thanks," Becky croaked. "Where's everyone?"

"Yossie's downstairs playing. Auntie Essie's gone home, she changed my bandages before she went."

"Didn't Mrs Lazarus come?" Becky asked.

"No, she didn't. Perhaps she was too busy and forgot."

"That's not like her. Anyway, I've got to go upstairs to tell Mirrie something, so I'll find out. Is Papa still upstairs?"

"No, he came back a while ago and then went off again to ask Moishe if he would help him make some stools for Mrs Lazarus. Her little business is growing, she needs more seating for her customers. Don't stay chattering too long, Becky dear. You look a bit flushed. I'll make you another honey drink when you get back."

★ ★ ★

Becky's head throbbed and her legs felt strangely heavy as she dragged her feet slowly up the stairs. She couldn't wait to tell Mirrie the news, she would be as excited as Becky was. The gossips in the public baths had been right all along about Mrs H. Dora had admitted that her mother was a bad cook; would Papa really change his mind about getting married when Becky told him? She knocked and waited, then knocked again. The next door neighbour opened her door and looked out.

"It's no use banging on the door, there's no one there!"

Becky frowned. "Perhaps they've gone to the market. I must have missed them."

The woman shook her head. "No, they didn't have time to go to the market, they were too busy. As soon as they'd cleared up, they packed their bags and left!"

★ ★ ★

Flat 74 Rothschild Buildings,
Brick Lane,
Whitechapel,
London.

Sunday 20th December 1908

Dear Mama,

I haven't written to you for weeks and weeks because I've been very ill with diphtheria. I don't remember much about it, except shivering one minute, sweating the next and crying with the pain in my head and my sore throat. I must have had a very high fever 'cos a bed was made for me on the living room floor near the fire as it was too cold in the bedroom. Yossie told me that Papa was so worried about me he sent for Doctor Simons, who arrived in his pony and trap! Now that's a piece of gossip which must have spread like a forest fire! The doctor charged two shillings and sixpence – that's half a week's rent! Papa must have borrowed the money to pay him. I think it included the cost of the medicine. It had such a horrible taste, I wouldn't have paid a penny for it!

Yossie had to stay at Auntie Essie's because diphtheria's catching. He was so good. He came every day, opened the front door a tiny bit and called out any news for me. He told me that on the day I got sick, Mrs Lazarus and Mirrie had rushed off to Liverpool for Mrs K's brother's funeral. When they got back, Mrs Lazarus and Auntie Essie took it in turns to nurse me. Mrs K brought food for Bubbe and at lunch time Papa popped in to see me and then went upstairs to eat with the young men. I missed Mirrie and Meg. I couldn't stop crying when they weren't allowed to come near me.

99

I look absolutely awful. I'm as thin as a poker and I've got blue shadows under my eyes. My face is the colour of putty and my hair is, well just ugh! I've missed a lot of school but I'll catch up, don't worry.

Now – for the Secrets Of My Heart. I think my being so ill stopped Papa from making any more wedding plans. It can't be long now because Yossie told me he's been to see the rabbi again. I still haven't been able to tell Papa about Mrs H and the cholent because I got sick the day Dora told me.

Very Special Secrets Of My Heart! Mrs Lazarus has been like a second mother to me. I wish she was and I wish I'd introduced her to Papa before Abe Klein changed our lives. It's too late now.

All my love, God bless.

Yours faithfully,

Rebecca Feldman.

Chapter 13

"Becky, look at this!" Meg stood on the stairs waving something in her hand.

"America! See?" she said, pushing a photo in Becky's hand. "It's Noo…something. I can't read the rest of it."

"It's a picture postcard of New York," Becky told her. "All those tall buildings are called 'skyscrapers' I think. Where d'you get it?"

"From the new feller what's just come all the way from America. Wasn't that kind of 'im?"

"I don't know who you mean."

"'Ershel they call 'im, I think. Yeah, that's right. 'Ershel."

Hershel! Becky felt the colour drain from her face. She'd forgotten all about him. "Has he come to live in England?"

"Dunno. I think 'e's got a room in the next building. But 'e's ever so nice, just like one of the family. You should see 'im 'elpin Mrs Lazarus dish out the dinners for the young men! If you ask me, I think 'e's very sweet on 'er," she grinned, giving Becky a knowing look.

"Sweet on her?" Becky repeated. "You mean…you mean?" she stammered.

Meg nodded, "No doubt about it. It's as plain as the nose on my face!" she said. "I'd best get a move on. Mrs Lazarus'll wonder where I've got to. Wait, just a minute, I forgot to tell you somethin' else. Guess who waved at me today?"

Becky shrugged.

"Your Dad!" Meg grinned. Wasn't that nice of 'im?"

"Was he going back to work?"

"Dunno. 'E was standing at the corner, talkin' to a tall man."

"Did he have a red handkerchief hanging out of his pocket?" Becky asked, dreading Meg's answer.

Meg thought for a moment. "Yeah. Come to think of it, 'e did. Funny lookin' bloke."

Becky felt crushed.

"You alright, Becky? You've gone all pale. What you need is a nice hot cup of tea to perk you up a bit. I'd make it for you myself if I wasn't in such a rush. I'll tell Mirrie I've seen you. She's a right good little 'elp to her mother. Bye."

So that's it, Becky thought, cupping her hands round her hot drink. *That's it*. Papa had been talking to Abe Klein, which means he's finally decided to marry Mrs Haffner. In spite of everything Becky had tried to do, it was all over. "Over," she whispered to herself. If that was the worst news ever, there was more to come. Hershel had come here to marry Mrs Lazarus; that would change everything. If he didn't want her to live with them, she'd have nowhere to live. All her plans had been shattered in one go. There was nothing left to hope for now. *It's all over, Becky Feldman, you tried your best, but it's all over now*. What was it that Hester had told her? "You'll just have to make the best of it."

She didn't know how long she sat staring into the fire, when suddenly, something seemed to snap inside her. Wild thoughts raced round in her mind. She sat up and took a deep breath. *No it's not over yet,* she whispered, *not yet, not yet!*

"Bubbe, I've just remembered something. I've got to go and see Papa. It's very important. It's about school," she lied.

"But you've just got in! Don't go out again dear, you've been so poorly and it's cold enough for snow. I can feel it in my bones. Your father'll be home soon, surely it can wait."

"No, no, that's just it, it can't wait!" She grabbed her shawl and scarf and was down the steps and running along the street before she could change her mind.

Bubbe was always right about the weather. Flurries of snow came swirling down from every direction and glistened in the light of the street lamps. Becky blinked as snowflakes brushed her eyelids and slid down her cheeks. The first layer of snow always reminded her of the smooth, white icing on a cake. Everywhere looked clean and bright, except for the grey slush splattering her skirt as the buses and horses and carts rumbled along the street.

She ran on and on until a stitch in her side forced her to stop. A small, scared voice niggled inside her. *You're crazy, Becky Feldman, and not only that, you're stark staring mad. Give up and go home.*

Just as she was on the point of turning round, her courage came flooding back. *IT'S NOT OVER YET* she shouted to herself as she pressed on. Papa would have to listen to her now, he had to. She didn't care what happened to her after that.

She banged hard on the door of the workshop and waited. She could feel her heart throbbing against her ribs.

"I've got to speak to my father, Jacob Feldman," she said breathlessly to the foreman. "It's very urgent."

"You'd best wait inside. I'll fetch him," he said.

Becky watched her father walking quickly towards her. He looked worried. "Right, Becky Feldman," she muttered through clenched teeth, "this is your very last chance!"

"What's the matter? Is Bubbe bad again?"

"No, she's alright. I must talk to you, Papa."

He frowned.

"What, now? Here, at work? Can't it wait until we get home?"

"NO, NO, NO!" she shouted. "That's the trouble. It can't wait. I must talk to you NOW!"

Without a word, Papa grabbed her arm and walked out of the workshop. They sheltered under the entrance porch.

"Papa," she began, her words tumbling out in a rapid torrent, "I know I shouldn't meddle in grown ups' business, but I've just got to. I'm nearly eleven and I understand things better now. I've got to tell you that Mrs Haffner cheated; she got someone else to make that delicious cholent, so you'd think she was a good cook. I hate Sol Haffner, he's a liar and a bully. I just couldn't live in that house after what he did to me. I wouldn't be able to work for a scholarship either and you know how much Mama wanted me to try for it. If you marry Mrs Haffner, I'm going to run away."

Becky stopped to get her breath back. She looked up at her father. His face was hidden in the shadows. She could hear him breathing quietly, but he said nothing.

"Papa," she went on, "I've lied, I've been rude and cheeky and answered you back and made you feel ashamed of me but...but it's because I have feelings, too. Mrs Haffner isn't like Mama is she? I'm sure you won't be happy and Yossie and me won't be either. I've tried so hard to tell you, but you never, never listen to me. Mrs Lazarus has been like a second mother to me, especially when I was ill. I...I switched the cholents that *Shabbos*, because I wanted to introduce you to her so I could go and live with her and Mirrie and Mrs K when you got married. When I saw that you both got on so well, I thought you'd want to marry her instead of Mrs Haffner. But now..." she choked, "but now," she went on, "everything's gone wrong. You're too late, Papa" she cried. "Meg told me that Mrs Lazarus's friend Hershel from America is very sweet on her. I think he's come here to marry her. If Hershel doesn't want me to live with them, I've got nowhere to go. Nothing ever seems to go right for me anymore, and...and...my boots are letting in water, and I'll get pneumonia and die and then you'll be sorry!" she sobbed, her whole body heaving and shaking.

Papa put his arms around her and hugged her close. He smelled of wood and sawdust. His wet beard brushed her face. "Shhh, don't cry, Becky," he whispered gently, trying to calm her, "don't cry."

She looked up. *Was his face wet with tears? Couldn't be. Must be the snow melting down his face*, she thought.

"We must go home. I'll speak to the foreman." Moments later he came out, carrying a clean sack which he draped round Becky's shoulders.

"This'll help to keep you dry," he said, keeping his arm round her.

They struggled along, heads bent low against the driving snow. Becky suddenly realised that Papa hadn't been angry. In fact he'd been kind and gentle after her outburst. He couldn't really have shouted at her when she was in such a state. Maybe she'd be in for it when they got home. She didn't care anymore. After all this time, she'd finally had her say.

Once inside the building, they passed their own door and went on upstairs.

"Where we going?" Becky asked, surprised.

"To Mrs Lazarus. I think she wanted to see you. Is that okay?"

Becky was too tired, too cold and too wet to answer.

Mrs Lazarus took one look at them dripping on the doorstep and threw up her hands in horror.

"*Oy vey*! Just look at you both!" she gasped. "You poor things! You must be frozen! Quick, quick, come inside. Take off your boots and wet things. Hershel," she called out, "put some more coal on the fire. Mirrie, get me some towels. Let me dry your hair, Becky. The tea'll be ready in a minute."

Later, when Becky was warm and dry, she looked around the room. Papa was sitting, like her, in stockinged feet, sipping hot tea and munching biscuits. He was talking quietly to Hershel. Had they met before? There was another curious thing too. Papa seemed, well, sort of comfortable, just as if he was at home. She couldn't make it out.

Mirrie's eyes were sparkling as if she was bursting with news. *Well, if it's about your mother and Hershel*, Becky thought bitterly, *I don't want to know. I wish he'd never come.* She bent down to examine a hole in her stocking. She sat up with a start when Hershel spoke to her.

"I feel I know you already, Becky," he smiled. "I've heard so much about you from Hannah and Mirrie."

Becky blushed. She didn't know where to look.

"We have you to thank, Becky," Hershel went on, "for

making us all so very happy. Your father must be very proud of you."

"Proud of me? Papa? I...I...don't understand," she frowned.

"I wouldn't have missed this happy occasion for the world," Hershel beamed. "I've just written to my wife to tell her the good news."

"Your wife?" Becky mouthed the words. Her voice didn't seem to be working.

"Oh, Hershel," Mrs Lazarus interrupted quickly, "you're confusing the poor girl. Let me explain my dear," she said, taking Becky's hands in hers.

"I came down to speak to you earlier on, but you'd gone out. Your Papa agreed that I should tell you and he has kept his word," she said, smiling at him. "Becky, your Papa and I are going to get married and...and I...we hope you'll be happy for us," she beamed.

"Hershel thought I'd already spoken to you," she went on, "so I can't blame him, but he's quite right, Becky," she said sweetly, "we do have you to thank for bringing us together! Switching the cholents was a brilliant idea!" she laughed.

Becky's mouth dropped open and stayed that way. She looked from one to the other in amazement. *They looked so happy, it must be true*, she thought.

"But, but..." she gasped.

"No buts, Becky, my very own matchmaker!" Papa laughed as he hugged her. This time there really were tears in his eyes. Tears of joy. "There really are no buts at all!"

★ ★ ★

Sunday 27th December 1908

Dear Mama,

At long last all my dreams have come true! Papa and Mrs Lazarus
are going to get married! I just couldn't believe it at first, but it's true.
We've all been laughing and talking, especially Mirrie and me.

Papa and Mrs Lazarus got to know each other after I'd introduced
them and during all those weeks when I was ill. Mrs Lazarus used to
come here every day and Papa too when he could.

Trust me to get everything wrong! I thought Hershel wanted to
marry Mrs Lazarus. I knew they were old friends, but I didn't know
he was married! He came over to see her and brought some insurance
money, whatever that means. I think her husband paid into some fund
and when he died the money was left to her.

Then I made two big mistakes. Papa met Abe Klein to tell him he
was going to marry Mrs Lazarus, not Mrs Haffner! The second was
about Rabbi Meyer, who asked Papa to help find a job for the father of
a poor Jewish family who had just arrived from Russia. It had nothing
to do with wedding plans between Papa and Mrs Haffner!

Mrs Lazarus wants me to call her 'Hannah.' She seemed to know
that I couldn't call her Mama. She said that a stepmother can never be
the same as a real mother, but she will love Yossie and me like her own
son and daughter. We just hugged and kissed each other and cried a bit
too.

We had a little party here this afternoon. Hannah looked radiant.
(A Miss Bennet word). She had her hair done up in coils on either

108

side of her head. Mrs Kaminsky, Auntie Essie and Hester have been mad busy baking. Bubbe helped a bit too. Mirrie and I borrowed plates and glasses from the neighbours and Meg came to help us.

"What's that everyone keeps sayin'?" she asked me.

"Mazel tov. That means congratulations," I told her. So she went round to everyone and wished them mazel tov. Meg's such good fun – a real godsend!

Papa and Hannah are getting married soon, before Hershel goes back to America. They want him to be one of the two witnesses at the wedding ceremony. The best news is that Hester is going to make new dresses for Mirrie and me. She's got some ladies' fashion magazines and we can choose the style! And guess what? We're going to have our very first pair of shoes! Well, we can't go to a wedding wearing boots can we? We're so excited. Yossie's happy too. Uncle Joe will make him a new jacket and trousers and Hannah has found him a very nice Hebrew teacher, so he doesn't have to go to that awful cheder any more.

Hannah wants to use some of her insurance money to rent a house. That way she'll have more room for her dinner customers. Mirrie and I will share one room, Yossie will have his own room and Bubbe will have one downstairs because of her bad legs.

I plucked up courage and decided to tell Hannah all about the hole in the herring barrel, 'cos it's always been on my mind. She asked me very nicely to apologise to Mrs Haffner, although it was a long time ago. I didn't want to, but I couldn't say no could I?

Mrs Haffner was very nice about it. She forgave me on the spot and immediately started to shovel some biscuits in a bag for Mirrie and me. She leaned over the counter and whispered: "At last Abe Klein's got me a good match. He had to go all the way to Manchester to find Morris. He's a widower from a good family. He's going to sell his shop and run this one for me."

We wished her mazel tov and just as we were going out of the door, she called out. "I've just got a new barrel of herrings in, Mrs Lazarus. Do you want some? For you they're half price!" Mirrie and I just managed to get out of the shop before we burst out laughing. Hannah said she was very pleased for Mrs Haffner, she hopes Abe Klein gets well rewarded for his trouble. He's earned it.

Now – for the Secrets Of My Heart. I'm not mad or anything like that, in fact I'm very happy, but isn't it just typical that the way things worked out with Papa and Hannah, I was the last to know!

God bless, Mama.

Yours faithfully,

Becky Feldman.